Edward L. Wilson

Mountain Climbing

Edward L. Wilson

Mountain Climbing

ISBN/EAN: 9783337287191

Printed in Europe, USA, Canada, Australia, Japan

Cover: Foto ©Andreas Hilbeck / pixelio.de

More available books at **www.hansebooks.com**

THE OUT OF DOOR LIBRARY

MOUNTAIN CLIMBING

BY

EDWARD L. WILSON   MARK BRICKELL KERR

EDWIN LORD WEEKS   WILLIAM WILLIAMS

A. F. JACCACI   H. F. B. LYNCH

SIR W. MARTIN CONWAY

CHARLES SCRIBNER'S SONS

1897

CONTENTS

VI

VII

LIST OF ILLUSTRATIONS.

Mount St. Elias and its Glaciers —

A Thousand Miles through the Alps —

MOUNT WASHINGTON

IN WINTER

By Edward L. Wilson

Mount Washington in March.

NINE months of the weather on Mount Washington are held in the clutch of winter. Nearly every day during that period, on its summit, or within sight of it, the snow flies. Its height is 6,286 feet above the sea-level. As Mount Hermon stands related to the Anti-Lebanon range, so stands Mount Washington related to our Appalachian Mountains; it is the Jebelesh-Sheikh,— "the old chief,"

—for it is nearly always hoary-headed, and its broad shoulders reach far above and beyond those of its neighbors.

The tens of thousands of people who visit its summit, after the tree-line is passed, see only a confusion of rocks on the steep inclines — naked, hard, sharp, time-worn, and weather-beaten rocks — on every side. If Nature ever tried to vary the scene by the power of her creative forces, the wind and storm have long ago mercilessly swept away every bush and blade, and torn loose every vestige of clinging moss and curling lichen. Only the barren stone and the detritus of centuries lie there, all as desolate as death. From the distance and from the mountain air the pleasure-giving comes. Only a few of those who have thus seen "the crown of New England" know anything of its winter glories; while fewer still have climbed over the snow to its summit. The day is coming, though, when the popular winter resorts will include Mount Washington, and the hotel on its summit will be well patronized by delighted climbers. For over a dozen years a winter visit was made less hazardous by the establishment of a United States Signal Service station there; for it was some moral help to the adventurous visitor to know that, should rough weather overtake him while making his explorations, he could find a place of refuge and a soldier's welcome until it was safe to make the descent. It would be madness to make the winter visit at the present time, however; for the government station has been abandoned, and there is no place of refuge there. When a better state of things prevails again, or when food and fuel are taken along, then it will be possible for others to share the pleasures and beauties I will try to describe — provided only, however, that a good supply of health, strength, and courage, sound lungs, a manageable heart, an experienced guide, and a cheerful method of taking disappointment, are also guaranteed. The weather and the condition of the highway vary; therefore cold and storm may change every plan, and close in upon every prospect of pleasure on the summit, after all the labor and fatigue of the climb are accomplished. Under such hard circumstances the philosophical mountaineer will form a plucky resolve to try for better fortune the next time winter comes along.

The best time to make the ascent is during the first week of March. Then the sun begins to play more warmly upon the snowy slopes, and the coolness of the nights forms a splendid crust upon which to climb. Moreover, less new snow is apt to fall after February turns its back. Of course the bare rocks afford better going than either crust or snow; but then, if the rocks were bare, it would not be Mount Washington in winter.

More than twenty-five years ago I met a friend who was just learning to focus a camera. I did not know much about photography or mountain-climbing then; but ever since we have studied their possibilities together, and they have drawn us into many a strange adventure. This weathering of so many years has strengthened a friendship which cannot be broken. I could not write what I have planned without associating the name of this friend — Benjamin W. Kilburn — with it. Together we have ascended and descended Mount Washington five times in winter. The glories and incidents of those bright spots in our lives I want to place on record, and illustrate some of them with the work of the third individual of our compact, — the camera.

The start was made from Littleton about seven P.M., March 2, 1870. The

The Last Half Mile — The Summit in View.

night was clear and cold, and the wind had fallen to a minimum. Through the long avenues of snow-clad evergreens we sped, getting out of the sleigh and trudging after it when we came to the higher hills, in order to make it easier for our willing horse and to warm our feet. How the frozen snow screeched as the sharp steel ran over it and cut it asunder! I think I never saw so many stars. They were un-dimmed by any intervening vapors, and they sparkled with unusual brightness.

Their light, caught by the freezing vapor which arose from the body of our little horse, formed a nimbus about her head; her nostrils seemed to send forth streams of phosphorescence as she sped along. It was so still too! The creaking and cracking of the ice, disturbed by the swelling of the Ammonoosuc from the melted snow which had been sent down from the heights during the day, and the ever-constant roar of the distant cascades, broke the quiet of the night; but everything else was still. The lights were all out, even in the camps of the wood-choppers by the way, and we seemed to have all the world to ourselves. It grew colder and colder as the three hours rolled by, and we found ourselves alternating with the lunch-kettle and a tramp after the sleigh to keep up circulation. It was a new experience to me, and sometimes I wished it was not quite so oppressively lonely. Just after we crossed the river we were startled by a crashing noise among the broken tree limbs which protruded from the snow. We had surprised a noble deer that was coming down into the valley to find water. As he disappeared into the forest he gave that shrill, defiant snort with which we were so familiar; and we felt that, having no rifle with us, we had

A Snow-storm below

missed one of the great opportunities of our lives.

To lessen the fatigue of the ascent, we planned to halt at the White Mountain House over night. It was ten o'clock when we reached there. We were not sure that even a watchman would be in the hotel at that season of the year, but we took the chances. After considerable pounding at the door, an upper window was opened, and a head appeared. It was evidently a dazed head, for in answer to our application for admission it said, "I guess I can't let you in, for the fires are all out and I am alone." Upon being assured that we both knew how to build a fire, and that we were not dangerous characters, the gigantic wood-chopper who had the place in charge came down to the door in his bare feet and admitted us; although, he averred, "it looked like a foolish kind of bizniss to try to go up that maountin." We thawed away his theories, however, and sealed a contract with him to "kerry" us to the base of Mount Washington next morning on his wood-sled, and to take good care of our horse until we returned. Then we "turned in."

Bright and early the logger's sled and two strong horses awaited us at the door next morning; and long before the sun rose, our faces were turned toward our far-away objective point. In less than an hour we came to deep snow, and the horses began to fret and flounder. At times the drifts were so deep that all hands were obliged to help shovel a way for the horses to pass through. Every mountain was shut in when the journey began, but when the sun came up the clouds grew uneasy and rolled about. At intervals they opened and revealed the snowy tops of the mountains, with the glorious blue over them. Then they closed in again, swathed the great domes, and drove the light back. The quick changes, with their strange contrasts, were exceedingly striking, and occupied our entire attention. With what systematic intermittence creation and destruction seemed to work! The clouds often hung like a tunic upon the mountains, with just their heads appearing; and then they would rise diagonally, like the knife of a guillotine, only to fall quickly, and cause the violent struggling and writhing to be repeated. At intervals the sun obtained the mastery, charging once more with his brigades and divisions; at the point of the bayonet he swept down the swaggering haze, and not even the smoke of battle remained. At rare moments it was beautifully clear, when a magnificent panorama was spread before us. In such sharp detail did Mount Washington then stand out, that, even with our experience, we fairly shuddered at the thought of climbing up its bleak and broken incline. The sun, acting like the developer upon the photographic plate, brought out the delicacies of light and shade with astonishing power.

As we approached the base of the mountain we found that a fresh, deep snow had fallen during the night, through which it was

Overlooking the Clouds.

impossible for the horses to pass. We sent them back to their stable, took to the snowshoes, and pushed on. It was then snowing hard, but there was nothing discouraging

about that. We knew there was a loggers'
cabin in the woods near the old railroad
depot, where we could rest and recupe-
rate. We reached it just as "John," the
caterer in the camp, had poured the water
on the coffee for dinner. We were invited
to partake of the humble meal of corn-
bread, potatoes, coffee, boiled pickled pork,
and black molasses. But I was too hungry
to depend on such fare, and secretly sneaked
out to the woodshed where we landed our
luggage, and made a requisition on the
lunch-kettle we had brought from Littleton. (It is only fair to the warm-hearted
loggers to say that when I returned from
the summit a few days after, I was so
changed, in some way, that I heartily
enjoyed their food.)

A consultation was now held as to the
propriety of making the ascent. "Mike,"
one of the sturdy woodsmen, said the
weather was threatening, "but we might
git up before the storm caught us." The
crust was all we could desire, as no snow
had fallen upon the mountain during the
night.

It was determined to push on and follow the railroad track, only diverting from
it when we discovered a better crust, or the
deep drifts made it dangerous. It was a

mercy to us that the sky was overcast, for our eyes were thus spared much pain. Mike accompanied us, " to help carry the traps," I was informed ; but in reality, as I afterward discovered, to help to carry me, in case I should " faint by the way-side." At first I was not allowed to bear any of the luggage. Even my overcoat was carried for me when the work grew warm. But as I displayed my power to endure, first my coat, then the lunch-kettle, and then portions of the apparatus, were gradually piled upon me, until I bore a full share of the load. The " wet " photo-graphic process was all we knew about then, and our developing-tent and appara-tus aggregated some seventy-five pounds in weight. Modern " dry "-process workers would abandon their pleasant hobby if forced to carry such a load as that. Noth-ing occurred to mar the pleasure of the climb until long after the tree-line was passed, and we came out into the " open country." The snow grew softer, even though the sun was not shining. When we could, we took to the rocks in prefer-ence. Sometimes they were slippery with ice, when it seemed wiser to walk around them and hold on to them. As to one walking along a muddy path, or over a pavement covered with slush, the opposite side ever seems the most enticing, and he, constantly changing his course from side to side, lengthens his journey with but little gain; so, when ascending a mountain in winter weather, one is always tempted to diverge from rocks to snow, and *vice versa*. Hands and knees were sometimes applied to the rocks. Occasionally a broad platform of clear gray granite afforded a place of rest and an opportunity to look down upon the white world from which we had risen. But when we turned toward the summit of the "chief," only gray clouds met the view. Not long before we reached the Half-way House an advance guard of great snowflakes came down upon us. They flew about as frantically as hornets. The wind became as fitful as a madcap, and drove us to the leeward of some of the higher rocks to escape the shaking it threatened. Now the snow seemed ground to powder, and was spurted into our faces with cutting force.

Then we entered a falling cloud, just as we veered to the right for the last long climb, when a cold northeast sleet-storm assailed us on the left. I never heard such a grinding din as wild Nature then made. We could not see a yard ahead, and the

Near the Tree-line.

noise was so deafening we could hardly hear each other speak.

"Keep the railway in sight, gentlemen, or we are in danger of losing our way," said the cautious Mike.

We were now perspiring "like August horses,"—on the side turned from the sleet. On the side toward the storm our beards were gradually lengthening to our

hips. Suddenly the wind grew more violent and erratic, and it became darker
than twilight. We could not stand alone.
Joined arm in arm, one following the
other sidewise, we made our way with
great difficulty up the now steepest part of
the climb. We had looked for " Jacob's
Ladder " as a landmark to guide us; but
the driving sleet hid it from us, and we
passed it by unwittingly. We bore to the
left to try to find it and get our direction;
but failing, we turned to the right again,
and tried to make a bee-line across the
great curve of the railway to the summit.
We floundered about there, confused and
bewildered by the storm, and were sometimes compelled to stop, bend forward, and
turn our backs until the gusts had spent
their strength. We were never cold, and
made up our minds to gather all the en-
joyment we could from this new experience. Many a battle with the elements
had been fought by us all in the days and
nights gone by, so it was now rather exhilarating than otherwise. The real danger of the situation, while it did not make
us afraid, caused us to cling closely while
we made one more effort to gain ground
against the storm.

" Mike, do you know where we are?"

" Yis, sur ; to an ell," he said.

What a noise was going on then ! A thousand whirling stone-crushers, with hoppers filled with the granite of Mount Washington, could not make a greater racket. What a giddy shambling followed Mike's last honest effort to bring us to a place of refuge! Suddenly we came into collision with an immovable body. The shock separated us. I saw a black, square something nearly facing me. Involuntarily I put my arms out, and made a desperate effort to embrace it. When I recovered I found it had embraced me. I had fallen into the open doorway of the old depot building, wherein was located the first signal station of Uncle Sam's weather bureau. My companions followed with less demonstration. In five minutes we stood over the government cook-stove, thawing out the icicles from our whiskers. The quarters of the observers then consisted of one room, with double floor and padded sides in the southwest corner of the building. Two stoves were used to keep the apartment warm, and very often they failed. Sometimes the wind drew all the heat up the chimneys as a cork is drawn from a bottle. We were made welcome by the observers, who were expecting us. I thought I had never seen so comfortable a place; but, in fact, I never passed so terrible a night. The great frame building rocked to and fro like a ship at the mercy of the sea, and the growling of the storm was more frightful than anything I had ever experienced on the water. The sleeping-places—deep, well-fastened bunks —were arranged at the south end of the room, one over the other, and were stuffed nearly full with blankets. Yet one could scarcely keep wedged in or warm; to sleep was impossible.

The ascents which followed varied but little in general method, except that the start was always made in the morning long before daylight; and good weather blessing us, as a rule, we were favored with such natural phenomena as come only in the mountains, and to those who love them enough to arise early in the day to greet them.

Our fifth and last ascent was made March 2, 1886. Modern inventions assisted. The " dry "-processes of photography were employed; and the journey to the base of Mount Washington was made, mostly before daylight, by the inglorious means supplied by a caboose on a lumber train. A deep snow had fallen upon the mountain the night before, so the ascent had to be started on snow-shoes. We followed the sled-road of the loggers for nearly a mile before reaching the railway. The trees were magnificently loaded. Falls and pit-falls were frequent as soon as we reached the mountain, because the new snow fell upon that which a rain-storm had soaked the day previous. Before we left the trees we heard a blast from an Alpine horn; and then we saw the great St. Bernard dog, "Medford," come bound-ing down

"*Medford*" *to the Rescue.*

through the snow, barking a welcome. He was our old friend, and very quickly secured the friendship of John's black Newfoundland by having a frantic tussle with him in the snow. Medford was followed by two of the members of the Signal Service. We had telegraphed our start from the base, and they came down to meet us. The snow-shoes were left at the tree-line, where we took to the rock and crust. But both were so despairingly wet and slippery that we left them and tried the cog-rail. It was too dangerously icy; so our last resort was the cross-ties, upon which there remained a few inches of new snow. Thus we ascended the rest of the way, helped by our alpenstocks each step in advance, straining and clinging and bowed down to the work. It required a desperate effort to hold our own against the wind betimes, and a continuously cool head was needed to grasp the situation. When crossing "Jacob's Ladder" we were compelled to resort to "all-fours," and more than once to lie flat and warmly embrace the ice-clad sleepers until the gusts had spent their strength. Taken altogether, this was the most difficult ascent we made. Aching muscles testified for a week afterward that snow-clad railroad cross-ties do not supply the choicest kind of going to the mountain climber.

It was fortunate for us that we did not plan to make our excursion three days

earlier, for on Feb. 27 one of the most violent storms ever known on the mountain took place. The "boys" thought
their last day had come. When we tapped
at the observatory door the sun shone so
brightly, and the air was so clear, that it
was hard to realize that it was ever any
other way there. We had often realized
differently, however. I must now turn to
the account of some of our experiences in
the neighborhood.

So restless are the elements on Mount
Washington that one must move alertly in
order to keep pace with the strange mu-
tations which they bring about. A sight
once lost is lost forever, for history is never
repeated exactly there. The usual excursions made by summer tourists are possible
in the winter-time. The "Presidential
Range" — Mount Clay, Mount Adams,
Mount Monroe, and Mount Madison, lying
shoulder to shoulder, apparently within
rifle-shot distance — affords a fine climb,
with better going than is possible in summer, provided there is plenty of snow.
Between it and Mount Washington lies a
ravine over a thousand feet in depth, which
bears the misnomer of the "Gulf of Mexico." Its sides are precipitous and rocky,

and the many springs which ooze from them supply the material for magnificent ice formations of varied colors. The tints are imparted by the mineral substances through which the streams find their way. It is " a spot of danger," and requires good courage and a faultless head to explore it; but the trained climber will like the excitement. When, now sideways, now grappling on "all-fours," and occasionally lengthwise, descending, you have gained the top of some great jutting rock, then lie down. Holding fast lest the wind catch you off guard, peer over into the abyss, and bear witness to the details of its wild environs. You will then believe any superstitious tale that is told you about the groups of demons which are seen dancing down there on moonlight nights, madly screeching in strange consonance with the roar of the hundred cascades at the bottom of the great pit. From a rock similar to the one I have spoken of, I saw a magnificent display of the winter forces one day. The exhibition began with a crash! crash! crash! underneath me. The time for the release of the stalactites hanging to the rock had come, and they started down the icy slope below. As the descending masses broke into fragments of color and rolled in

Tuckerman's Ravine, from Mount Washington.

the wildest confusion down, glittering in
the sun, the scene baffled description. A
channel was cut through the ice and snow
deep into the side of the ravine; the moving mass then started on every side a can-
nonade of rocks which was simply terrible.
Enough ice was wasted to make a million-
naire — sufficient granite was torn to fragments to build a block of New York flats
— all rattled down into the gulf at once
with maniacal fury, as if their mission
were to burst the sides of the great gulf
asunder. Some of the masses of ice striking rock or crust, rebounded like bil-
liard-balls, and, whizzing in the sunlight,
glistened like massive diamonds and ame-
thysts and emeralds afire. The horrible
grinding of the rocks amid the dust of the
snow was even more exciting. Sometimes
the rock masses overtook one another in
the air, and by the awful collision reduced
each other to small fragments. The line
of fire was wide enough to sweep a bri-
gade of infantry from the face of the
earth. How still it was when the last
projectile had spent its force against the
rocks far down in the depths of the gulf!

Such exhibitions are liable to occur on
a March day, when the sun shines; and
they make the descent into the ravine dan-

gerous, unless the shadows are resorted to for protection.

The wildest place of all the surroundings of Mount Washington is the well-known Tuckerman's Ravine. It affords grand opportunities in winter for witnessing some of the most curious meteorological phenomena. In five minutes after the summit of the mountain is left you are out of sight of all the buildings thereon. The confusion of rocks is the same in every direction, and you are in chaos. The brisk cannonading I have described is of frequent occurrence here; but even more mysterious is the manœuvring of the clouds. Witnessed from a good stand point far down in the ravine, on a favorable day, nothing could be more grand. Boiling and seething, they rise and ride and drive without apparent purpose. I have seen the great masses separate, and one section continue on its hasty journey, until, as though realizing its loss, suddenly it would stop, then go back, make fast to the lost section, and continue on its course around or up the mountain. Sometimes the wind tears the great gray masses asunder, and carries them in various directions as easily as a spider hauls a fly across her web. When they have reached the places willed by the in-

visible power, the detached masses are sent
whirling about the neighboring mountains,
as though in search of some lost member
of their force.   In the summer-time they
are not so placid as in winter, for the rat-
tling thunder accompanies such contentions
almost any time after the mercury reaches
" sixty above."

On a cold day, when the clouds have all
been sent on distant missions, and no haze
obscures the view, the side of Mount Washington toward Tuckerman's Ravine resembles a steep cathedral roof, with thousands
of buttresses as white as the finest Carrara
marble, and as glittering as the alabaster
of the Nile.   After a new snow on such
a day, and with the right sort of wind, the
most wildly exciting of all exhibitions takes
place.   The snow begins, with an ecstatic
gyration, to rise from the crest of the ravine
in the form of a slender column. It gathers
body as it rises, and, like the clay in the
hands of the potter, seems to swell as
though it was a cylinder, and the snow
was rising inside it, increasing its diameter.
How it spins — then struggles — then with
awful speed approaches the verge of the
ravine, and leaps out into space.   Only a
little imagination is needed now to picture
the monster reaching out its arms franti-

cally, and shrieking. It hangs aloft for a moment, trembling and vibrating; then the wind receives it in its broad lap, and with relentless hand sows it broadcast over the terrible ravine. One after the other the snow monsters quickly follow — down to their doom. Thus snow-squalls are born, and thus the depth of snow to a thousand feet is packed down in the bottom of Tuckerman's Ravine to shape the great "snow-arch" which so many visit every summer.

Every day new experiences, always marvellous, may be had when the storms permit a visit to these deep places. It is never safe to go down into them alone, unless calm and clear weather are assured. You may feel that your experience has enabled you to place all confidence in your own eye, in judging of snow and slide, and in unravelling the time-worn and time-scarred passages; you may feel satisfactorily conscious of the power of your strong arms to hack and hew your way through difficulties; memories of former tastes of the glorious luxury of being entirely alone, where all nature is beautiful, may tempt you; but at high elevations in winter you should draw the line. Self-reliance is a good element, but it is always best to pool your supply with another of equal mettle. You take your life in your hands when you attempt "snow-work" alone. A misstep may break a leg or hold you fast. Yet, battling with the elements on Mount Washington is the most exhilarating exercise one can take — with wise precautions. A journey down to the "Lake of the Clouds" gives the wind a fair chance at the ambitious climber, and is a fine experience. The broad expanses on every side cause one to shudder at the thought of being driven down one of them with no power of resistance. In the coloring of the air, so peculiar to this westerly side of the mountain, and in the grandeur of the great sleeping masses which lie down toward the Crawford Notch, and upon which the colors fall, no matter when you look upon them, you are sure to find revealed grand features that lift up your soul to a new majesty.

A much more picturesque series of excursions is afforded by the "Glen" carriage-road. At night and day, a visit at any lookout on this road well repays for all the labor entailed and for some measure of risk. On a clear day, when the sunbeams glide over the peaks and up the valleys, unrestrained except by the broad

The "Presidential Range" and "Gulf of Mexico," from Mount Washington.

shadows of the mountains, the distant views, all the way down "to the earth," are very fine. Toward evening, or close on to a storm-coming, the gauzy haze begins to soften the outlines and dilute the coloring of the mountains. Then the mist, rising and thickening, joins forces with the wind, and the creation of the most peculiar of all the results of the cold begins. I allude to what the observers

term "frost-feathers." I have often stooped
to "talk" to tiny ones in the Alps, but I
believe they are not known elsewhere as
large as those found on Mount Washington. The absolute transformation brought
about by them is bewilderingly lovely.
One hour after the wind has driven every
vestige of snow from the summit, and the
buildings are as clear of snow as when
newly constructed, they may all become
covered with frost-feathers so profusely
that every rigid outline is gone, and every
object appears like a confused mass of
eiderdown. More than three-fourths of
the time the summit is cloud-enveloped,
on account of the warm air which arises
"from the world" and condenses overhead.
When a certain degree of humidity is
reached, the mist freezes the instant it
touches anything. We will suppose that
the wind drives it against a telegraph-pole.
A frozen layer is deposited upon this, and
is instantly followed by another and another, until, if the wind does not change,
a "feather" branches out horizontally
from the telegraph-pole until the strange
creation points out into the air, one, two,
three — five feet or more. Over this and
under it and alongside of it, other formations go on, shaped like the wings of sculp-

tured angels, or like the tails and wings of doves in the old-time tomb-marbles, every bit as pure and white and soft as alabaster. Their growth is very rapid. If a flat surface is chosen by the eccentric sculptor, then the feathers radiate irregularly from a central point, and are moulded into fascinating patterns as delicate as fern leaves and the feathers of birds, and always at an angle over each other. They are not like ice or snow or frost. They bend like tendon, and they are as tough as muscle. When melted, the most pure water possible is the result. Where fractured, their glistening, granular substance looks like marble or alabaster. Everything becomes covered and coated by them. When you tread upon them they are found to be elastic, and a peculiar nervousness takes possession of you. A latticed window covered with them is more charming than an Arabic Mashrebeyeh screen, with its delicately pierced patterns and its intricately chiselled bars. The feathered side of a tall rock appears like an obelisk high in air; every inch is hieroglyphed by deep-cut characters, which, though beyond the ken of your philology, are full of meaning, and make plain a lesson of the beautiful. As soon as the wind changes, these lovely creations droop, drop, and disintegrate, while others form in their places, always on the windward side of the objects which they choose to glorify. Never does the summit of Mount Washington and the objects about it appear in such imposing glory as when lustred by frost-feathers. If you will walk back of the signal station on a moonlight night, before the moon is very high, when the frost formations are favorable, and look down the railway, the draped telegraph-poles will resemble a procession of tall spectres—or, if you choose, monks or one-armed dervishes, half in shadow and half in the glittering light, marching to the shrill fifing of the wind, or gliding along with the rich contra-basso which comes up from the wide mouth of the ravine. What a bejewelled world it all makes!

If there was no other diversion on Mount Washington, watching the intermittent extinction and generation of the clouds affords sufficient interest to occupy much of the time. There are "best days" for this, however, as well as for the other sights. The summit of the mountain must be clear, and the sun should shine brightly. Then, if a snow-storm forms, say a mile below, one of the most enchanting of all natural convulsions delights the observer. The unsubstantial formations rival in grandeur the solid mountains themselves. Disturbed by the warm air below them, and chilled by the cold blasts above, the great seas of vapor begin to roll and tumble and pitch, until a regular tempest forms, and sways them all. The billows form great swells and depressions. They break angrily against the rocky mountain, and their snowy spray flies high in the air. Rising and falling, twisting and tangling, they tell of the falling flakes and grinding snow-dust with which the earth is being visited. The more the commotion, the more active is the fall going on below. How they toss and tumble, and how magnificent are the changes of light and shade!

I witnessed the finest show I ever saw of this nature one afternoon, about half an hour before sunset. The great orb seemed to sink into a sea of saffron; yet it shone with almost painful brilliancy. Suddenly upon the cloud surface in front of my standpoint, a mile below my feet, a great mass of shining light appeared. It was as brilliant as the sun, and of about the same color. It was a " sun-dog," — the image of the sun reflected on the white bosom of the snow-storm. It remained in sight for some time, and was caught by the camera. The snow-storm continued, and the sun departed amid an attendance of clouds equal in glory to any summer sunset I ever saw. The coloring upon the upper surface of that raging snow-storm was beyond the gift of the painter to counterfeit. As soon as its life went away the stars began to appear, for night comes quickly. I heard a great screech down in the valley, and saw a tiny glow coming toward me, like a "will-o'-the-wisp." It was the headlight of a locomotive on the Grand Trunk Railway at Gorham. Then the nearly full moon grew stronger; and a vast triangular shadow of the mountain was projected upon the cloud surface, black and solid and threatening, where but a few moments ago I saw the boiling color. Soon the snow-like sphere cleared the mountain-top, and all space on every side was illuminated down as far as the clouds. But they continued to boil and drive and snow.

From a point opposite I have watched the clouds at break of day, and have tramped my circuit in order to keep warm while the process of sun-rising and cloud-dispersion went on. Few have ever beheld such transcendent glory at sunrise as Mr. Kil-

burn and I did one March morning from
Mount Washington.   At first the cloud
masses seemed to reach from us, ninety
miles, to the Atlantic, over Portland way.
A crimson glow, blended into orange and
gray, then arose like a screen — a background for the enchanting scene which
approached.   The clouds grew uneasy at
this, but joining forces, resisted, and for a
time hindered, the progress of the drama.
Then yielding, they separated here and
there, and we could, with the field-glass
we had, catch glimpses of light through
the rifts.   The earth was in full sunshine.
We saw the streets of the villages.   Men,
pygmy - sized,
were shovel-
ling snow, and
tiny horses and
sleighs passed
i n s i g h t.
T h e n t h e
clouds shut
in, and the
m o u n t a i n
was in twi-
light once
more.   A
great cloud-
parting took

Frost Feathers. Tip-Top House.

37

place, and the mass below us broke into a thousand fragments. These gambolled and rolled wildly from side to side, and carried with them fragments of gaudy spectra which resembled broad segments of rainbows. Every moment there was a change of form and color. Again through the rifts we saw the world. Now the many tints became more scattered as the clouds rose with the light, and interfered with its course. Only the snow-storm equalled the billowy confusion — nothing ever equalled the coloring. At last a gleam of light shone in the observatory window, and caused our sleepy hosts to turn under their blankets. The sun has risen on Mount Washington.

Another phenomenon I witnessed once only. It began between ten and eleven A.M., and lasted almost an hour. At first a great, broad, gray ring, quite luminous, appeared around the sun. It was a "clear" day, but the firmament was scarcely blue. A secondary ring, as large and as broad and nearly as luminous, formed, with the sun at its eastern edge and half within the ring. At three other points of this ring, and with the sun dividing it into four equal segments, were "sun-dogs," very bright, with a prismatic corona around them.

One of the ordinary diversions " on the hill " is to stand on " Observatory Rock," west of the signal station and just a little below, to see the great pyramidal shadow of the mountain cast by the rising sun on the snow just before the rosy glow comes shooting over the frost-feathered ridgepole of the Signal Service station. It is as black as the shadow of the real pyramid cast by the sun or moon upon the yellow sand of the desert of Gizeh. When the atmosphere is sufficiently clear, as it frequently is, the mountains nearly a hundred miles away appear sharp and near. The whole White Mountain range is unobscured.

"Oh, the mountains! the mountains!" exclaimed my enthusiastic companion, when we witnessed the last sunset together there. " I never saw them look as they have looked to-day." This was an oft-repeated saying, but it was always true ; for in fact the mountains never appear two days the same. Either sun or storm, or cloud or the seasons, or all combined, work up a composite for each day, always full of character, but never twice alike. Therefore the mountain-lover, unlike the fisherman, is "always in luck." He always finds " peace, beauty, and grandeur " harmoniously blended ; and he is ever " brimful of content." Whether breasting a storm or standing victorious upon some hardly-gained height, he is always sure to be repaid well for all his endurance by the glories which surround him. Truly has that stanch climber in the Alps, Professor Tyndall, said : " For the healthy and pure in heart these higher snow-fields are consecrated ground."

Almost every one is familiar with the duties and the functions of the observers of the Signal Service. But on Mount Washington their duties are peculiar. Seven observations must be made daily. The recording-sheet of the anemometer must be changed at noon. Three of the seven observations must be forwarded in telegraphic cipher to the Boston station. Routine office-work — letters received and sent — must have attention between-times, and several blank forms must be filled with statistics. The battery and the wire of the telegraph plant must receive careful attention, and the matter of repairs is no inconsiderable one. The station on Mount Washington is the bleakest, and, with one exception, the coldest, in the service. Three to four men, including a cook, are usually there, with one cat and one dog.

Sunset. A Sun-dog on the Snow-clouds

Life would be very hard to bear there, were it not for the click! click! click! of the telegraph instrument, which is the active connecting link with the world — the mainstay and hope of these recluses. And then flirtations with the world's operators is a necessity. A regular consternation occurs in camp when a storm breaks the wires and connection is lost. In such cases the observers risk their lives in storm and cold in search for the break, rather than be without the assurance of safety which the click seems to impart. The men live on as good food as can be. The larder is supplied in September, and the "refrigerator" (the top story of the observatory) is stocked at the same time. Meat and poultry are placed there already frozen, and they do not thaw "during the season." The water-supply comes from the frost-feathers. Care is taken that two or three barrels of these are stored in the back shed always, and a boiler full of them in half-melted condition is ever upon the cook-stove. A water famine has been known to occur, when from the oversight of the cook the supply of frost-feathers has been allowed to go down, or " poor weather for frost-feathers " comes along. A drink of this all-healing feather water can always be found on the stove, icy cold, if the cook attends to his duty.

A hurricane at sea is hardly less frightful than a big blow on Mount Washington. I was literally blown out of bed one night. I was about to accuse my bedfellow of kicking me out, when instantly he came following me. The grind outside was frightful. We knew the airy structure was cabled and anchored to the rocks by ship's chains; but they seemed to expand so that it shook like an aspen leaf, and creaked like an old sailing-vessel. The wind tussled with the double windows, and capered over the roof like a thousand ogres. There was no sleep for any one when there was "such a knockin' at de do'!"

Morning was always a relief after such a storm, even if it brought no cessation and but little light. Sometimes the feathers so obscure the windows that the lamps must be lighted in daytime. At other times the wind tears so through the building that the lights cannot burn. With all the fires going the mercury has been known to fall 23 degrees below zero inside the observatory. On Dec. 16, 1876, the temperature outside fell to 40 degrees below. The mean temperature for the day was 22.5 degrees below. The wind was at

80 miles at 7 A.M., 120 miles at 12.22 P.M., 160 miles at 4.57 P.M., 100 miles at 9 P.M., and 180 miles at midnight. The force of the wind was terrible; and at times masses of ice were blown loose, making it extremely dangerous to stand under the lee of the building. The window on that side was fastened with planks in case of accident.

One of the greatest storms ever known occurred in February, 1886. The mercury dropped to 51 degrees below zero, and the wind rattled around at the rate of 184 miles an hour. It tore down one of the buildings, and fired its parts against the observatory, threatening to break in all its doors and windows and the roof. But the stanch little building had a tough, thick coating of frost-feathers then, which proved to be a real protection to it, and so escaped. It was no pleasant task, however, to sit there and hear the twisting and crunching of the timbers of the neighboring building as they fell a prey to the angry elements. The anemometer on the roof was carried away from its bearings that night. A few days afterward a similar storm came up, but not quite so violent a one. Mr. Kilburn and I made the ascent the day before. A strong rope was tied around the waist of Sergeant Line when he climbed to the roof to make his afternoon observations, with all but one of us anchored at the other end of the rope. The camera caught him in the act. The wind-cups of the anemometer were spinning around so they could not be seen with the naked eye; and yet in the photograph they plainly show as a blurred circle, or resembling more a tube bent into circular form.

But for these excitements "the boys" would suffer from *ennui*. They insist that their life "on the hill" is not the most happy one in winter. It has frequently been broken into by sorrow and sadness too. One observer died there, Feb. 26, 1872; and his companion was alone with his dead body for two days before the storm would allow any one to come up to him. A coarse coffin was made, and a rude sled; and then a solemn procession moved slowly down the mountain-side, over the snow, that the mortal remains of a brave boy might be deposited under the earth.

It was a matter of "turn" with the observers who should go to the base periodically with and for the mail. These journeys were often attended with much peril, and necessarily were frequently pro-

longed so as to cause much anxiety. The
relation of one such incident will suffice to
show what it meant sometimes to be a
member of the Signal Service stationed on
Mount Washington.

Never was there a kinder heart engaged
in the service than that of Sergeant Wm.
Line, now (1891) stationed at Northfield,
Vt. (where he died in 1895). He served
on Mount Washington for quite five years
(from 1872 to 1877), and I met him
there several times. As near as I can remember them, I will in his own words relate the story of what he considers his most perilous ascent. It occurred on Nov. 23,

Measuring the Wind.

1875. The day was unpromising. Against
his judgment he left Fabyan's at about nine
A.M., with the mail accumulated, for the
summit. The team engaged to take him
to the base could only pass a little beyond

Twin Rivers, so from there he took to the snow-shoes. Arriving at the base, he found every building deserted. At eleven A.M., without a word of cheer from any one, and alone, he began the ascent. The old Waumbek Station-house was passed, and the foot of "Jacob's Ladder" was gained in safety after two hours of pretty hard work. The snow was then three or four feet deep, and the gusts of wind began to increase in power and in frequency. A few steps only could be made in the lulls between the gusts. When the hard blows came he was forced to lie down until they had gone over him. An hour was consumed in climbing the next half-mile. When the Car House (used for storing tools and railway appliances) came into view, Sergeant Line tried to reach it. A gust carried him to the railroad track. He caught the T rail in his hands, when his body was blown up against the cross-ties, and held there for some time. The next lull allowed a little progress; and the Gulf Station-house could be seen, but it could not be reached. Said Sergeant Line : —

"I found I was being swept rapidly toward the Great Gulf, so I floundered myself over against a rock, and succeeded in coming to a halt. After resting a while, assisted by my pike-pole, I tried to reach the house ; but it was impossible. I could not breathe facing such a wind; so I lay down, and, feet first, backed up the snow-drift which had piled up near the building. Such procedure was slow, but sure ; thus the house was reached. I could not see it; but I knew when I had reached it, for I fell about six feet down the inside incline of the drift, and brought up at the house. The wind had driven the snow clear away from the building, all around it, for some distance. I was unharmed, and quite content to be out of the power of the wind. At three-thirty P.M. I started on the journey again, having recuperated my strength in the house. Hardly had I opened the storm-door when it was banged shut again with such force as to break it in two. The wind subsided somewhat in an hour, when I made another start. After many efforts I gained the top of the bank of snow, only to be whirled back, and lodged under one of the supports of the building. I concluded it was useless to try to reach the summit before night; so I returned to the house, and gathering what wood I could, I proceeded to make a fire. When prepared to strike a light, to my horror I found my match-box was gone. It had rolled out of my pocket during one of my tussles with the wind. A frantic search revealed in my vest pocket a single match, which had been given me in the morning with a cigar. It was damp; but knowing that my life depended upon it, I carefully dried it between thumb and finger, and with anxious heart tried to ignite it. Gentle frictions gradually restored it — it ignited — I was saved. At seven P.M. I had a good fire. I found an old teapot containing some tea that was steeped four months before. It tasted like turnips. But with it, and some cakes Mrs. Line had put in my knapsack in Littleton, I made a fine supper. I was tired by my day's work, and soon after I fell asleep. It was seven A.M. before I awoke. In a few minutes after I was on my way again. I was making good progress, and was near the summit, when I met my companion, Mr. King, coming down the mountain to search for me. I am sure he was glad to be relieved of a great anxiety, such as we had all shared in the past when searching for the bewildered and the lost. Hardly had we reached the platform in front of the hotel on the summit when we heard voices. Immediately three men appeared

Valley of Ammonoosuc.

coming up out of the fog. They were
Mr. B. W. Kilburn of Littleton, and
Messrs. Band and Gallagher. The last
two had been requested by Mr. Kilburn
to join him in his search for me. He
had been awakened near midnight by the
telegraph operator with the intelligence
that I was lost on the mountain. Immediately and alone he started in his sleigh
for Fabyan's, travelling all the rest of the

night in the storm and cold. From Fabyan's he walked to the base. He lost his way once in the meadows before reaching Fabyan's, as it was then so dark, and so rough was the storm. He searched the mountain for me, and saw where I had rested on the way. Had he been an hour earlier he would have passed me while I slept. No one appreciates better than I do what heroism it required to undertake such a search. While we breakfasted together, and related our experiences, an inquiry came from headquarters at Washington as to my whereabouts. In a few minutes after a message from Littleton came, announcing that six men had left there to help Mr. Kilburn. Then a third message reported that the railroad company had detailed fifty men, with pick and shovel, to search for the man who was lost. But my brave friend headed off all these generous enterprises by quickly returning to the base with the intelligence that the lost was found." *

Many times the observers risked their own lives to rescue the perishing. A telegram was always sent from Littleton when

---

* The Government signal station on Mount Washington having been abandoned, a winter ascent should not be attempted without a careful guide.

any one started "up the hill;" and if a
fairly prompt arrival was not made, a
searching party was at once sent out from
the observatory. Help from Littleton was
also called for. Brave hearts always re-
sponded promptly in such cases.

One descent, which I shall describe, was
eventful, and typical of all the similar journeys I had made. With long, swinging
strides we started down the slope, crushing
at every step enough beauty and glory to
excite the wonder and admiration of the
world. The sky was blue, and the wea-
ther-makers promised us a "clear day."
The dawn had developed into glorious
morning, and the sun was pouring its
libations of gold and purple over the
mountains and down into the frozen valleys. Again we saw the loftier heights
tinged with rosy hue, while the limitless
shadows which fell upon the snowy slopes
caught and repeated the soft azure of the
sky. The crust was hard, the rocks were
glacéd, and long fields of ice stretched between them, which made the descent a
dangerous one. We passed from snow-
crust to ice, and from ice to rock alternately. The thin ice upon the rocks, over
which the melted snow had trickled the

day before, was the most troublesome, and required great caution. Once with my alpenstock I made a mighty advance-lunge at such a rock, in order to obtain a stop for breath when I had leaped upon it. Alas! the ice was not so thick as I had anticipated. The steel point glanced, and my staff went from my hand, leaping through the air, and ringing like a bell as it went. I soon forgot my loss in watching its strange antics. For a moment it glided over the broad ice-slope below, half erect; then it fell and bounded up and down like a rod of iron, until, striking another rock end first, it came up all standing again, then again flew through the air as before. It turned and rolled over, and shifted end for end, slid sideways, bounded and leaped, gaining speed as it went, far away from my recovery. The last bound I saw it make was into a ravine. Fortunately we had bound duplicate staffs upon our shoulders, so that no inconvenience followed the escapade.

Seeing a wide field of ice below us, and which we must cross, we halted upon a broad-topped rock to take breath and to tighten our luggage before we attacked it. We had passed the frost-feather line now, and the rocks protruded more nakedly through the snow. As we looked back, there was a noble amphitheatre with clean-swept stage. The crags and spurs supplied the accessories; the backgrounds and screens were of light and shade most mysteriously composed. In all positions the actors stood, some in simple garb, others with costumes laced delicately and embroidered fantastically by icy needles in hands more deft and skilful than ours. It was a gorgeous scene. How many storm dramas had been enacted there !

But there was a difficulty behind us, and we must turn and face it. It

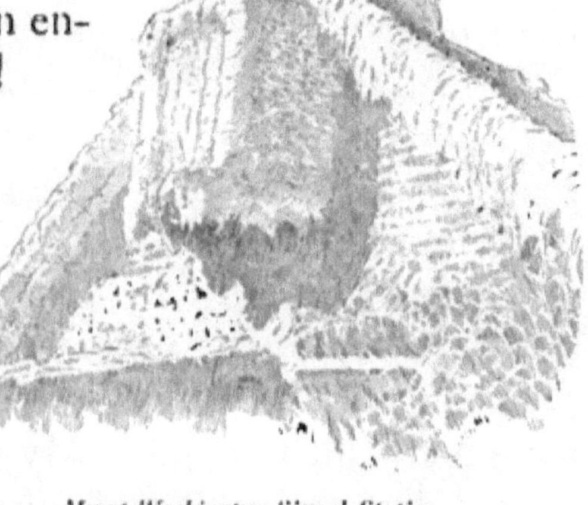

Mount Washington Signal Station.

was an ugly spot, and neutralized the pleasure of examining the surroundings somewhat. We made up our minds to glissade the slope, and glissade we did. Before we began, my careful companion gave me this piece of advice: "Keep your mind wholly upon your feet and upon your staff. Press down upon the first with all your might and main, and have the other every instant of the time in good position to press it down, hard, in case you fall. If you slip, turn quickly upon your face, sprawl all you can, to make yourself as wide as you can; push the point of your staff with both hands hard into the ice under you; this will probably stop you. Under no circumstances allow yourself to slide on your back." I did not slip until I came within a few feet of the foot of the slope.

Instead of obeying the rules, I allowed my mind to rest upon embracing a narrow rock ahead as soon as I came to it. I came to it, face down, sooner than I calculated. The heavens scintillated while I dreamed, and when I came to my wits again I was lying on my face astride the narrow rock for which I had aimed. My plan had succeeded, but the ways and means employed differed somewhat from the details of my drawings. Glissading is an upright and manly diversion — at least it should be upright — but success does not always crown the first attempts at it. The start should be made with the alpenstock held firmly in both hands, and trailed after you at one side. Do not allow the head to change places with the feet; resist all intimacy on the part of the ice. Have no collision with it. The stars belong to the heavens, and should only be seen with the eyes cast upward. Do not sit down to work, nor "take a header" willingly. Press the steel point of your staff vigorously into the ice, if you falter, and secure a soft place for recuperation before you fall.

Perhaps if I had not been thus brought to a stand-still we should never have obtained the sublime views we had over the bristling trees across the country and down into "the lower regions," as the observers say. Turning our eyes to the summit we saw veils of thin clouds winding around the mountain in folds which excited our æsthetic fervor. Then they thickened into long furrowed lines, dark and threatening, and these began to roll and toss about. "The whispering grove betrays the gathering elemental strife," the book of "Weather Proverbs" used by the Signal Service says. The truth of this was verified to us now, because, as if in sympathy with the disturbance gathering about the summit, the groves a half-mile below us began "whispering" ominously. We knew what it meant. The sky was yet clear,

but the wind began to blow furiously from
the west-southwest. It had been snowing
from there down to the base for two or
three days, and we no sooner left the ice-
slopes than we had to meet the deep drifts.
The great trestles of the railway were
snowed full, and we dared not try descending on them. For descending they are
always dangerous. We had to flounder
through the deep snow the best we could.
We could not make our way to the little
tool-house where our snow-shoes had been
left. Up to the waist, then, we plunged.
Our progress was very slow. It grew suddenly much colder, though it was below
zero when we started. The wind increased
rapidly, and came in thundering gusts.
From the rising snow-columns we could
see the gusts coming. Before they reached
us we locked arm in arm, turned our backs,
bent forward, and allowed them to sail over
us. Gradually our mustaches froze over
our mouths, and our eyes were sealed so
we could not see. Frequent halts were
made to thaw in some daylight, and secure
breath. Sometimes a treacherous drift led
us to an icy bottom, when we slipped, and
became almost buried in the snow.

The contest for position in this world
was reins-trying, but we thoroughly en-

joyed it ; and more tears and frozen eyes were caused by our laughter than by the snapping irascible wind and cold. Once in a while, when I squeezed the arm of my companion, with whom there was no fear necessary, he would reach his spare mittened hand to his mouth, thaw out his voice, and say, "Do not be afraid, I am right here by your side."

Frost Feathers under the Railway Trestle.

It is always safer to go around a mountain drift than to go over it. Only long experience enables one to understand when it is safe to attack drifted snow. It is at times very treacherous. It may slip while you are pushing your way over it, and, avalanche-like, rush down some steep incline with you; or, it may have become separated from the rocks which it covers, by the melted snow running underneath on warm days, when it is liable to crush in with you and overwhelm you. It is a good plan to test it with the alpenstock before risking life upon it. With my experienced friend I never felt that there was any danger of going into a pit unless he went too. His strong arm has rescued me from danger many a time, and as frequently has he carried me over the rough places on his shoulders. There is a great contrast in our make-up. He, broad and strong and muscular as an ox — I, tall and slender, light-weight and wiry. Both had attained a quick and springy step, and a mutual trust had sprung up between us which made it out of the question for one to oppose himself to the other in time of peril.

At last we reached the woods, and hugged as closely to the railroad as we could; for now and then the wind had cleared a sort of " path." But the frequent pitfalls twisted our legs and bruised our feet, so that as soon as possible we turned to the right, and made our way down into the sled-road, then in use by the

wood-choppers. One time I took a run
down a slope which seemed to have a crust
upon it, but presently I broke through
and fell forward. As I yielded to circumstances, I intuitively put out my hands.
They went into the snow up to my shoulders, and there I had to remain, face down,
"all-fours" fastened in a drift more than a
dozen feet deep, until Mr. Kilburn came
to my release. Soon after we heard the
ringing of the woodsmen's axes; and in
twenty minutes more we were at the base,
safe and sound. It was like a spring day
there. The little river, cajoled by the
benign warmth of the sun, had burst its
bonds, and piled the "anchor-ice" several
feet high on either side. Countless rivu-
lets of melting snow were pouring into it.
The commotion was almost equal to that
at the mouth of an Alpine glacier. It was
like the closing of some magnificent scenic
opera. The soft, sweet music caused by
the explosion of the bubbles bewitched the
air. Each swollen, sparkling stream came
along charged with individual ring and
resonance — each one came cheerily to
contribute its melody to the orchestral tu-
mult farther on.

SOME EPISODES

OF MOUNTAINEERING,

BY A

CASUAL AMATEUR

By Edwin Lord Weeks

*The Peak of the Zinal-Rothhorn from the Hörnli.**

" Think of the people who are ' presenting their compliments,'
and ' requesting the honor,' and ' much regretting,' of those that
are pinioned at dinner-tables, or stuck up in ball-rooms, or cruelly
planted in pews — ay think of these, and so remembering how
many poor devils are living in a state of utter respectability, you
will glory the more in your own delightful escape." — EOTHEN.

EFORE venturing to touch
upon a theme which has
already been treated by able
pens, and to add a few personal impressions, it may be
as well to call attention to the fact that
much of what has been written hitherto
is addressed to those technically familiar
with the subject, rather than to the general
public.   It is only fair to admit that popular opinion is divided as to the attractions

* The illustrations of this article are all drawn by the Author.

of one of the grandest of open-air sports, which in sustained interest and variety of incident is second to no other. There are hopeless but well-meaning sceptics, who will ask one: Why take the trouble to climb a peak in order to see a view which can only be enjoyed for a few minutes, if at all, by reason of cold or fatigue ? and it is not easy to convince them, since seemingly unnecessary physical exertion does not enter into their ideas of pleasure, that the contemplation of nature, however impressive it may be, is not the sole object and end of the climber ; and that the interest, the charm of the thing, as in art, lies not so much in the subject as in *the way it is done*, in the hundred incidents of the route, and, above all, in the joy of life and the new vigor born of exertion in the bracing air of high altitudes, which are the reward of a successful season.

September, 1893.

I.

THE statements of Baedeker, as to the relative difficulty of certain peaks, may, upon the whole, be accepted by amateurs with confidence. In the editions of " Baedeker's Switzerland," a few years ago, there was a list of the principal summits about Zer-

matt; and among them a group consisting
of the "Ober-Gabelhorn," "Zinal-Rothhorn," "Weisshorn," "Dent Blanche,"
and "Dent d'Hérens" was prefaced by
the lines, "very difficult" (for thorough
experts only with first-class guides), and
not "altogether free from danger." In
the most recent edition this last clause does
not appear, from which circumstance it
might be inferred that with the progress
made by the Zermatt guides in the science
of climbing, and with their ever-increasing
experience and topographical knowledge
of these peaks, the actual danger has been
sensibly diminished.

But the amateur who has already had
some experience, and is confident (but not
too confident) of his own powers, and is
moreover in good condition, need not allow himself to be daunted by Baedeker's
classification. Among the minor peaks,
(minor, not in regard to size or interest,
but in difficulty only) the Rimpfischhorn
and the Gran Paradiso are ranked as difficult. Both of these peaks exceed the
Jungfrau in height; and although care and
attention are necessary at certain points,
there is not the slightest difficulty about
either of them. A noted Alpinist records
that he has ascended the Gran Paradiso

Peter Taugwalder, No. 2.

alone and without guides. There is one
point, however, where most men would feel
safer with a rope, and at least one guide. A
practised expert whom I met on the way
down affirmed that it was hardly worth
doing, while another, equally experienced,
had made the ascent twice. As for the
Rimpfischhorn, it shows, on a small scale,

examples of the various difficulties common
to all rock peaks, and with but one guide,
"strict attention to business" is necessary.
Although one of the noted Zermatt guides
who accompanied the writer on a rather
more trying expedition, declared it to be
simply "une jolie promenade," others consider it one of the very best peaks for pre-
liminary practice, before undertaking more
hazardous ascents. Of those classified as
"very difficult," I can speak from personal experience of only two, others having
proved to be impossible at the particular
moment when they were attempted; and
although sufficiently arduous, these two do
not offer any insurmountable difficulty, so
long as one is not subject to vertigo, that
nightmare of all beginners, and has sufficient imitative faculty to follow the movements of the guide in front. It is a very
important point at the outset to save one's
strength; for even should he have a super-
fluity of endurance, he had better store it
up for emergencies. Any one who takes
notice of the gait of the guides when starting at night by lantern light, will observe
that they walk with a long, swinging,
rhythmic step which seems quite mechan-
ical, as they slowly lift one foot or swing
it over a rock, with scarcely any expendi-

ture of force, particularly in mounting the
tedious moraines where the bowlders are
often white with frost. All the energy
thus economized comes into play when
one reaches the rocks, where a man wants
a clear head as well, and to know just
where to rest his weight to take advantage
of every projection, point, and crevice.

For amateurs whose object is not so
much to make a record as to obtain the
greatest amount of sport with a moderate
expenditure, the high glacier passes afford
nearly as much interest as many of the
well-known peaks where the tariff for
guides is much higher; some of these
passes cross ridges or "saddles" from
twelve to fourteen thousand feet above
the sea, and have the additional attraction that every step of the way is new,
as one descends into another valley at
night, where the French or Italian inn
replaces the Club hut which he left at
daybreak. And there are some which are
really more dangerous than the majority
of peaks; as, for instance, the "Altes
Weissthor," from Zermatt to Macugnaga.
I have never crossed this pass, but once
had a good view of it when descending
the New Weissthor, a short distance away.
While we were breakfasting on the brink

Zinal-Rothhorn — Sunset.

of the cliffs an avalanche fell directly on the route, which is seldom free from falling stones; and yet the tariff is only forty or forty-five francs for a guide, while eighty is demanded for the Jungfrau! And there is also the Col du Lion on the Matterhorn, which offers similar inducements. Then

there is at Randa the Domjoch or the
Mischabeljoch, neither of which is much
inferior in height to the great peaks on
either side, and both lead down to Saas-
Fee by descents of uncommon steepness.

It has been a fashion, particularly of late
years, for experienced Alpinists to make
difficult or little-known ascents unattended
by guides; and while experience and self-
confidence may be better acquired in this
way, they are often dearly bought. Accidents have happened to the most famous
experts while prospecting alone; and it will
be found that by far the greater number of
Alpine catastrophes have been due to care-
lessness, and to the rashness of novices in
venturing too far without guides. Unless
one is extremely quick and clever, he is
very likely, when he finds himself in a
perplexing situation, to under-estimate the
difficulty of certain passages, where danger
is not apparent, but which a guide would
never attempt; such, for instance, are the
steep and sunburned grass slopes high on a
mountain-side, which often terminate in
cliffs or vertical ledges above a glacier. As
the tufts of dry grass usually point downward, they afford little hold to the nails in
one's boots, and are often as slippery as
glass. There are also certain places which

look appalling to a beginner, but which turn out to be perfectly easy when once the guide in front has got safely over them. Most treacherous of all to the solitary climber are the steep *glissades* * down couloirs of snow or ice; and a little accident which happened to a friend of the writer, although he fortunately escaped serious damage, had the effect of making him forever after over-cautious in regard to this extremely rapid but uncertain mode of progression. While waiting at Pra-Rayé, at the head of the desolate Valpelline valley, for settled weather in order to cross the "col" to Zermatt, he left his guides at the chalet, and ventured on a little private exploring expedition up the unfrequented Glacier de Bella Cia, near the Château des Dames. He had taken an alpenstock belonging to his porter, one of the slender tourist sort, branded with names; and as he turned back to descend, he concluded to pick his way down a long slope covered with loose rocks and *débris*, which seemed a more direct route than the break-neck ledges by which he had scrambled up. The slope descended steeply,

* The sitting *glissade* is perhaps the most exhilarating way of getting down a long snow-slope, such as the one on the Dom, and does not call for the same degree of acrobatic skill as the standing glissade.

without a break apparently; but as he got down, the valley beneath him seemed to retire by some unaccountable effect of aërial perspective, which made him suspect the existence of a precipice invisible from above. Proceeding cautiously downward, he found himself on the verge of a long and vertical ledge, and keeping on along the brink he finally reached a steep *couloir* or narrow chasm filled with packed snow, which offered a short cut down between jagged walls of rock. As the inclination at which the *couloir* descended did not seem dangerously steep, he attempted a standing *glissade*, using his stick as a brake in the usual manner. It became steeper as he slid down; and in trying to check his velocity the stick snapped in two, and he shot down the incline feet foremost with the speed of a rocket. Luckily the chasm made a turn at right angles, and he was landed on a heap of stones, with no further damage than the loss of considerable epidermis, and the annihilation of his trousers.

To-day, when every great peak has been thoroughly explored, when famous climbers have achieved the most difficult summits alone, or at least without professional guides, but few remain the mere ascent of

A Ladder of Ice — Zinal-Rothhorn.

which confers any brevet of distinction in
this field of athletics. As in all professions
and in all sports which boast semi-profes-
sional experts, the standard has been raised.
In order to take a high rank, or to "make
a record," the aspirant for the honors of
the Alpine Club must traverse such peaks
as the Matterhorn, and descend on the opposite side, or cross the Dom du Mischabel,* the highest peak on Swiss soil, which
presents little difficulty until one descends
the steep rock face above Saas. There are
still a few summits left which are admitted
to be somewhat "tough," and one of the
most successful enthusiasts in the matter of
rock peaks has recently given his verdict
in favor of Chamouny as a happy hunting-ground; for he found sufficient interest in some of the slender *Aiguilles* which
surround Mont Blanc to stimulate his
somewhat jaded appetite. It would, however, be quite incorrect to make an arbitrary statement that any particular ascent
is easy or difficult. With bad weather any
minor peak may become hazardous at once,
or when a fierce gale of wind whistles and

---

* According to Baedeker's figures the three highest summits
of the Alps are Mont Blanc, 15,366 feet, Monte Rosa, 15,217,
and the Dom du Mischabel, 14,941. The first belongs to France,
the second is on the boundary between Italy and Switzerland,
while the third alone belongs entirely to the latter country.

howls among the rocks as through the rigging of a ship, and they are crusted with *verglas* or frozen sleet; it is only just, therefore, to say that the expeditions referred to here were nearly all made under favorable circumstances.

II.

While detained at the Eggishorn hotel by bad weather, in 1886, I picked up a copy of the *Times*, or some other London daily, and found an editorial relating to a recent accident on the Dom du Mischabel, and it also contained a letter or statement in regard to the claim put forth by an Englishman who had just made the ascent, as he believed, for the first time; this presumption was contradicted by others, who claimed to have made prior ascents. I have since seen guides who thought that it had been done as early as 1865. In those remote days the Dom was invested with imaginary terrors, and a certain prestige, like that of the Matterhorn before Mr. Whymper made the first ascent, although of course in a lesser degree; at that time there was no cabin, and climbers were obliged to pass the first part of the night under the cliffs above Randa.

Now that the Dom has a Club hut, and the route is well known, it presents no difficulty, although rather long and tedious, rising, as it does, more than ten thousand feet sheer above Randa. The day which we chose for the trip was the first on which it would have been feasible, after a long period of bad weather with much snow, and we overtook several other parties on the road. The great rampart of tawny cliffs above the valley, which forms the pedestal of the Dom, rises to such a height that one can see nothing of the glaciers and peaks above them. In the centre, and at the bottom of this amphitheatre of cliffs, there is a cavern, probably an extension or widening of a deep cleft which was cut through by the torrent issuing from its mouth, and which trickles across the broad delta, or sloping plain of gravel and *débris*, at the base. When we had crossed the torrent at a point far below, and were ascending the steep pastures beyond, toward the cliffs, it was our good fortune to behold the most magnificent of avalanches. The stream where it poured out from the cleft began to rumble hoarsely, raising its voice to a sullen roar, while the water changed to snow and ice, ever increasing in volume

The Ascent of the Dom — the start at 3 a.m.

until the whole broad slope was deeply
covered with a fast-moving white carpet,
over which great blocks of snow and ice
chased each other, leaping into the air,
and breaking as they fell into showers of
fragments and frozen spray. Seen from
below, it must have resembled the coming
of a tidal wave. The ascent of the cliffs
was facilitated by two or three long ladders placed against their most vertical portions; but we had the blazing afternoon
sun of August on our backs, and were
sufficiently hot and thirsty by the time
we reached the top, and could look across
the icy desolation of the Festi Glacier to
the vast bulk of the Mischabel group rising beyond it. Some English Alpinists
had already installed themselves at the
new Club hut, and were luxuriating in
iced wine punch, which had been prepared in a flexible canvas bucket; and they
held it out to us, as we arrived, hot and
breathless. Certainly nothing ever looked
more tempting than its crimson depths,
with the lemons and blocks of ice swimming about; and even the strictest Mussul-
man might well have been pardoned if for
once he forgot his creed, and looked upon
the wine when it was red.

The cabin had a sloping platform for

sleeping purposes, extending along the wall for its entire length on the side opposite the door, which was well covered with clean straw and plentifully provided with blue blankets, each marked with the C. A. of the Club Alpine. There was a large stove at one end of the narrow space left, with a table and a few wooden benches near it; and at the other end a primitive stairway led to the loft, which was sacred to the guides. When the numerous and cosmopolitan company had tucked themselves away in the straw at the early hour of 8 P.M., the cabin presented a droll appearance, with its long row of heads, variously nightcapped, each emerging from its blue blanket. Although at such an elevation the nights are usually cold, on this particular night a blanket was quite unnecessary, and the fleas, which are never absent from the clean straw of Switzerland, were uncommonly active; there was also a man who snored, and two or three who told stories. As there was little prospect of sleep, I wandered out in search of a cool spring which bubbled up at a little distance from the door, and which could only be found after much groping and stumbling among the rocks. There was no moon; and while the ground underfoot was

The Over-Gabelhorn.

almost un-
distinguish-
able, the vivid
starlight made all
the encircling peaks
clearly visible. Just
across the deep gulf of
Randa, which had the
blackness of a pall,
arose the colossal bulk
of the Weisshorn ; and
the white chaos of se-
racs and glaciers lead-
ing up to it seemed to diffuse an almost

phosphorescent glimmer, while from behind the black pyramid of the Matterhorn the Milky Way rose straight toward the zenith, like a flaming sword. The dead silence would have been oppressive, had it not been broken now and then by the muffled roar of a torrent somewhere down below, which came at intervals on some stray current of air, like the hollow rumble of a distant train. In the dry night wind at this elevation, there is a subtle quality which makes one feel so keenly alive, that only a modicum of sleep is necessary ; and one is loath to exchange its freshness for the close, stove-heated air of a *cabane*. And if one remembers for a moment the Turkish proverb which, as everyone knows, runs thus, "A man is better lying down than standing, sleeping than lying down, dead than sleeping," it is only with the impatience of the scoffer at a philosophy with which he cannot feel in touch. At one o'clock, after we had all dozed a little, there was a sound of heavy boots coming carefully down the stair ; and presently the guides were all at work heating *bouillon*, or making coffee over the stove. The first to start was a German with two guides, and we followed shortly after ; by the time we

had picked our way by the light of the
lantern over the bowlders of the moraine,
and along the crevasses of the glacier, we
sighted his lantern, which shone like a
star, high up in a *couloir* of snow leading
to the *arête*.   Here we overtook the German, and after a consultation our guides
thought it advisable that we should all be
roped together.   We had not proceeded
far along the wedge-like snow *arête*, which
leads, if I remember rightly, in an almost
unbroken line to the summit, when we
came to the only break in its continuity,
a huge and jutting promontory of rocks,
which seemed to cut the *arête* quite in
two, and to bar our farther progress.   The
German team in front, like ants when interrupted in their travels by any obstacle,
kept straight on, and scaled the cliff, but,
when they reached the summit, seemed
unable to get down on the other side.
My guides, seeing their predicament, unharnessed themselves; and we started round
the ledge on the side, where it rises above
the Festi glacier.   One by one we worked
along the wall until we came to the corner.   The first guide had already turned
it; and, having need of both hands, I was
beginning to find my piollet somewhat
embarrassing, when we were nearly toma-

hawked by the piollet of one of the men over our heads, which he had dropped in his struggle to get down. As we ducked instinctively, another piollet whizzed past like an arrow, and buried itself in the ice of the glacier far below. It must have taken them nearly an hour to recover their lost property; and, after regaining the snow *arête*, we continued serenely on until we neared the apex of the Dom, where we were the first to arrive, between seven and eight A.M. As we neared the summit, ledges of rock arose through the crusted snow on the Zermatt side; and the ridge, ever steeper as we toiled breathlessly upward, rose before us like the razor edge which all good Mussulmans must traverse if they would reach Paradise. But from the top of the Dom it was the majestic triple peak of the "Gran Paradiso" which we saw rising over the shoulder of the Matterhorn, but far away on the Italian side. It is said that from this height the Mediterranean is often visible; but although the sky overhead was of the deepest and most cloudless blue, the nearer snows dazzling, and the long white chain of the Oberland toned by a golden haze, the plains of Italy beyond the lakes faded away into a vaporous horizon on the south.

As we turned to go down, we met the others coming up along the ridge; but our guides, for some good reason — probably the steepness of the crusted snow slope — preferred to take a different route, and, turning to the right, we sat down in the snow, and slid or *glissaded* down what would make the finest and dizziest of toboggan slides, to the valley at the foot of the Taschhorn.

Although the Dom is undoubtedly one of the finest of the great snow peaks, the ascent of it does not present the varied interest of

*Peter Taugwalder, No. 1.**

many rock summits far inferior in height; and the only amusing bit of rock-work which I remember, is the passage of the ledge or cliff near the beginning of the *arête*.

* The numbers 1 (above) and 2 (p. 68) are given, not in order to discriminate in favor of one or the other, but are a means of identifying them, as they are namesakes. Peter Taugwalder, No. 1, is one of the survivors of the famous Matterhorn disaster in 1865, when he accompanied his father as porter.

III.

The Val d'Aosta, as one leaves Courmayeur and Mont Blanc behind, opens below like the portal of a new world, and is a charming interlude between the arctic world which we have just left and that which we are to encounter on the other side of its high mountain wall. The green vineyards of Italy border the dusty highway, and each jutting promontory of rock is crowned with a castle or watch-tower. Near Villeneuve, on the south, is the narrow entrance of the gorge which leads upward into the Val Savaranche, which is one point of departure for the Gran Paradiso region. When entering this valley for the first time, I had come up from Turin and Cuorgné, by the "Col de la Croix de Nivollet," and by way of Ceresole Reale, entering the Val Sava-ranche at Villeneuve. I reached the little hamlet of Pont, a scattered group of weather-beaten chalets at the head of the ravine, late in the afternoon. An old *garde-chasse*, wearing the badge of the King of Italy on his hat, met me on the road, and proffered his services as guide, as he had a key of the Cabane on the Paradiso. We

put up at a cantine, the nearest approach
to a hotel in the village, which was kept
by a most obliging woman, surrounded
by five or six tow-headed children, who
sprawled over each other in front of the
great open fireplace. For other furniture
the room had a pine table with a bench
on each side, a spinning-wheel, and two
or three closets in the wall, where our
hostess kept her crockery and supplies of
chocolate, sardines, and other luxuries for
improvident pedestrians. Her cuisine,
naturally limited in this bleak region, included soup, eggs, and chickens, of which
a goodly number strutted in front of the
door, or foraged on the kitchen floor, so
that without leaving her fireplace she could
pounce on the chosen victim at the proper
moment. But this time we were doomed
to disappointment; the weather changed
for the worse, and, after passing a night
in the loft overhead, where, although the
beds were sufficiently immaculate, there
was hardly room to stand upright, we were
obliged reluctantly to abandon the trip; a
cold storm had set in during the night,
and the heights around us were hidden by
the driving rain. My second attempt, although it did not begin as auspiciously,
ended in the most satisfactory manner.

The old *garde-chasse*, when I reached his house lower down in the valley, was away hunting steinbock* with the King; and I could find no one to take his place in the village of Pont, when I arrived there for the second time. There was still an hour for a little prospecting before dark; and hoping to get a view of the hitherto elusive Gran Paradiso, I kept on to the end of the valley, and turned up the bridle-path which leads to the cabane. But the great summit is not visible, either from this valley or from Cogne, being environed by a circle of lesser satellites which are yet high enough to cut off the view entirely; and it is only from the heights around Zermatt that one can get a satisfactory impression of the highest peak in Italy.

The cabane, having been designed as a royal shooting-box, is superior in its equipments to any Club hut with which I am familiar, and is approached by a well-kept bridle-path, which winds upward in long zigzags. When turning to come down, I saw far below, at the foot of the cliffs, a party of three, who were on their way up, carrying a coil of rope and various other

---

* The adjacent hills, as well as those around Cogne, are still the haunt of the steinbock, or ibex, which are reserved for the exclusive sport of royalty, although the chamois are free to all at the proper season.

A Long Step — on the Gran Paradiso

impedimenta. They proved to be two
young Italian engineers, accompanied by
a guide whom they had engaged for the
season; and with the amiability characteristic of Italian Alpinists, they invited me
to make one of their party, only stipulat-
ing that I should bring up provisions and
a few extra metres of rope. They were
to sleep at the cabane, and start at five in
the morning. It was then about six P.M.;
and I was not long in getting down to the
cantine, swallowing a hastily cooked dinner, and securing a supply of provisions.
Our hostess found the rope, which was
crammed into a sack with the rations; and
her husband, carrying a lantern, officiated
as porter. The Italians were already asleep
when we reached our quarters, which were
truly palatial for a "hut" at this elevation;
the room which they occupied opened into
a large dining-room furnished with a long
table and chairs, and beyond this we found
a kitchen, a room for guides, and another sleeping-room provided with several
bunks and mattresses. A single figure was
stretched out in one of the bunks, and the
room was heated by a drum connected
with a stove in the adjoining kitchen. I
was rather too hasty, however, in congrat-
ulating myself on such unwonted luxury;

for the temperature of the room, uncomfortably hot when I turned in, became chill and frosty when the fire had gone out, and it was not until my room-mate shook himself out of bed at the call of his guides, that I discovered that there were blankets, and that he had appropriated all of them, my share as well as his own. Taking advantage of the unusually complete cooking facilities, and the generous supply of crockery provided by royalty for hungry Alpinists, we dallied late over a rather elaborate breakfast; and it was broad daylight when we struck into the path, and began to clamber over the frost-covered bowlders which lead up to the snow-fields. In speaking of a path here and elsewhere, I refer always to the distinct foot-path, which, in the case of mountains frequently ascended, leads from the starting-point, Club hut or inn, up the moraines to the glacier. Beyond this point there may exist, during a long season of fine weather, traces in the snow left by the last party, which, of course, are obliterated by the first storm. The only other landmarks or indications of human life above the rudimentary path up the moraine and the occasional tracks in the snow are the deposits of broken bottles and

empty tin cans at points where the guides
are in the habit of stopping. In cases
where the ascent is not often made, these
indications are not to be depended on.
As there was only one guide and no porter
in this party of four, the provisions and
other baggage were divided, and each man
carried his share of the weight; mine, in
addition to my own personal belongings,
was a bulky wooden wine-flask, of a make
only found in this part of Italy, and large
enough to supply the entire party. The
weight was of little consequence; but its
size and bulk were rather in the way when
we got to the rocks, and more than once
I was nearly carromed off a cliff by its ro-
tundity. While we travelled along the
snow-ridge, and the first ice-slope where
steps were cut, our guide did not think it
worth while to put on the rope; although
we struggled along one after another, and
a decidedly rapid toboggan slide led down
to the edge of a cliff overhanging a glacier
which we could not see. An icy wind
blew down the slope, and the slowness of
our progress upward did not tend to increase our somewhat sluggish circulation.
The first striking feature of the route was
a long *Bergschrund*, or horizontal chasm in
the ice, fringed with pendent icicles, and

of varying width, which must first be crossed before we could mount the steep, snow-covered dome on the other side, which led to the ridge of rocks at the summit; this was the most toilsome part of the ascent, as the beginning of the slope directly at the edge of the crevasse had the bulging outward curve of a Persian dome. The ice was covered to the depth of a foot or more with loose snow, which had to be scraped away before the steps could be cut. As it happened, none of us were properly equipped for the occasion; the guide had the only piollet, the rest of us having alpenstocks, and my one pair of woollen gloves did duty for three, each taking his turn. In consequence of our improvidence, one of the party had the hand in which he held his staff so shrivelled by the cold wind that for months afterward it had a shrunken look, although not actually frost-bitten, while the fairest of the two Italians suffered from sunburn to such a degree that his face was puffed out with water-blisters; he had rubbed it with butter before starting, but far from impeding the action of the sun-glare, it seemed rather to increase its effect, so that he became a sorry spectacle on the following day. As for the guide and myself, our weather-beaten hides were too well tanned to suffer much from a little additional exposure. Subsequent experience has taught me that one can never consider himself exempt from sunburn; and in going over tracts of newly-fallen snow, and when the sun shines through thin vapor, what is called a "white mist," very few escape entirely.

Having reached at last the top of the snow-dome, we found ourselves near the rocky ridge backbone which crops out through the snow at the summit of the Gran Paradiso; it had a strikingly artificial appearance, and might be likened to an old Roman wall, while the three tall aiguilles, one of which is the true summit, heighten the resemblance still more by looking as if built of superimposed blocks of stone. When we had clambered up to the top of the wall, which was at least five or six feet broad, we walked easily along, sometimes climbing over a large block of stone covered with snow, until the thoroughfare came to an end at the foot of the first summit. Here we saw that it would be necessary to pass round the outer wall, which descended quite vertically for some distance, until it reached the snow-slopes and seracs which led down to the glacier. Our guide went first, showing us that there was in reality no difficulty about this *mau-vais pas*, which at first sight did not look invitingly easy.   We all held him by the rope, while he worked along the face of the wall, clinging to the projections, or searching with his fingers for the crevices, and then with a long step across space (I cannot remember now how far down the slope began, but the impression that there was both space and depth was vivid enough at that moment) he reached a sure foot-hold in the rocks of the second " chimney," and then we all followed one after the other.   My turn came last, and being slightly embarrassed by the wine-flask, it was necessary for me to hug the wall closely ; then with a brief scramble up the rocks we reached the summit.

Nowhere among the Alps is there a panorama of more impressive desolation than this.   In almost every similar prospect, even the more extensive view from the Dom, the eye may travel downward without hinderance, from the Switzerland of the Alpinists to the deep grooves haunted by summer tourists — the green valley with the railway track along the bottom, the great hotels — and one may imagine, if he cannot see, the long procession of pleasure-seekers, each carrying, ant-like, a burden of some sort. But here the connecting links are missing; there is no populous valley just below, no summits seem to overtop us but the distant snows of Mont Blanc and the "Grand Combin," and nothing meets the eye but the world of ice and rocks, and solitude, which shuts out the nether world.

Josef Marie Perren (Guide at Zermatt).

Here on the summit one of the Italians had an ill turn, which might have been mountain sickness, or it may have been caused by indigestion, and it was evident that our guide felt some anxiety about getting him down along the wall; but after he had slept for half an hour in a sunny nook the feeling passed off, and we reached the cabane without further difficulty.

On the following morning we started for Cogne by the Col de Lauzon,* a charming

* Col de Lauzon, 9,500 feet.

route, from the forest of fir and larch above
Pont to the high green pasture slopes, and
over a rocky saddle, where we had a capa-
cious lunch. While we lay smoking on a
flat rock in the sunshine, and sheltered from
the wind on the " Col," a single chamois
wandered across a patch of snow far below
us: we all shouted at once; and he disappeared with a few leaps, followed by eight
others. Down among the green slopes below we came to a hunting-lodge belonging
to the King, and late in the afternoon we
reached the little town of Cogne. The
villagers were all sitting and gossiping on
their doorsteps when we passed through,
as it was Sunday afternoon, and the blond-
haired peasant-girls were in holiday-attire ;
all wore high white ruffs, like those in portraits of the Medici period, long-waisted
bodices, and short skirts of some dark blue
material, relieved by narrow strips of col-
ored silk.

There were two hotels in the village,
and one of my companions said that they
were going to the " Grivola." He did
not like to recommend it, as it was kept
by his cousins, and he even admitted that
it was considered dearer than the other;
but we went to the " Grivola " notwithstanding. The sign-board swung in the

wind at the end of a long iron bracket, and the whitewashed stone walls were pierced by small grated windows, a prevalent fashion in Cogne, which gives to the place something of the character of a Spanish village. Within, there was a long dining-room with quaint old furniture, and quainter engravings on the white walls. In the travellers' book a noted climber had recorded his ascent of the Gran Paradiso without a guide; it may have been easy enough for him, but the casual amateur would feel more tranquil with some one at the other end of a rope.

Here our friends were made welcome, and we all had a huge supper. Roast chamois was one of the principal dishes, and the wine of the Val d'Aosta was poured out by a girl with a Medici ruff. After coffee in the morning my bill was a trifle over five francs, all included; but possibly the other hotel may have been a shade less expensive.

IV.

THE Zinal-Rothhorn or "Moming" is, to use an Anglo-Indian phrase, a "puckah" mountain, which means that it is the real thing, and not a sham; it holds a very respectable rank among the local aristocracy of rock peaks, the crowned heads which rise above the high white ridges surrounding Zermatt. Although we found no unusual difficulty on the Rothhorn, there was too much snow near the summit, and the ascent was long and fatiguing; but a quiet gray-haired lady who dined at the *table d'hôte* at Zermatt had made the trip three years before, and did not seem to consider it by any means an unusual performance. Her companion, who was my neighbor at dinner, told of a man who, without much previous experience, had chosen it for his first essay in climbing. When he had reached the peak, with its shelving slabs of rock, and ladder of ice, he lost his head entirely, and the guides were obliged literally to carry him down, one of them placing his feet in the right spots, and the other holding him by the shoulders; this is a fine illustration of the strength, coolness, and pluck of these men.

Before attacking the Rothhorn we had sustained a defeat, or, rather, we had made an ignominious and perhaps unnecessary retreat the day before. We had first undertaken the " Ober-Gabelhorn," which, although not quite as high or as expensive, is at times even more difficult. After passing the night at the " Trift " inn, two hours

above Zermatt, we were obliged to give up
the trip, as the weather had changed. We
made a second expedition to the Trift on
the following day, and at two in the morning we set out for the Gabelhorn again.
Pietro shook his head doubtfully when he
saw the quantity of snow on the rocks, and
seemed reluctant about starting. During
the halt for breakfast, at sunrise, on the
rocks below the Gabelhorn glacier, we
were joined by an English climber with
a " record " and a vigorous pair of long
legs. He had just come up from Zermatt without stopping at the Trift; and
although his guides, who were both young
and ambitious, seemed very doubtful about
the success of the undertaking, he decided
to keep on as far as possible; and we all
began the ascent of the glacier at the same
time. As we got higher up, the soft snow
covering the ice-slopes became deeper, and
Pietro became more despondent. Both of
my guides finally halted, and declared that,
although they were willing to keep on, they
considered it a useless waste of strength,
and were quite sure that it would be impossible to reach the summit in time to
return before nightfall. Yielding to the
advice of the older and more experienced
guide, we turned back, not without regret,

and concluded to devote the remainder of the day to prowling about on the lower summits, and to attack the Zinal-Rothhorn on the following night, as it appeared to be in better condition, and less buried in snow. We had not proceeded far in our descent, looking back from time to time at our friends, who were still struggling upward through the deep drifts, when Pietro was seized with the qualms of indigestion, which accounted, in a measure, for his reluctance to go on. It is quite impossible for any man, however strong, to climb rocks when suffering from even the least touch of dyspepsia; one might as well engage in a prize-fight with a broken wrist.

It was not until five o'clock in the afternoon that our friend returned to the inn, just as we were thinking of sending up after him, and narrated over his tea, and in a voice as husky as my own at the moment, how they had at last reached the " Gabel " after unusual exertion, and in spite of the overhanging cornices of snow, they had clambered up to the summit. The guide, who was still suffering from indigestion, was replaced by Peter Taugwalder (No. 2), and by two A.M. we were toiling up the steep and seemingly endless moraines below the Rothhorn glacier.

Now, while we are still half awake, and not wholly reconciled to being up and astir, it seems a fitting moment to make the admission that one of the least attractive features connected with the assault of any respectable peak, is the unearthly small hour at which one is routed out of bed, and compelled, for the sake of prudence, to swallow a substantial meal. When the previous night is passed on the straw of a "Club hut," one may sometimes look forward to early rising without regret; but when, as at the Trift, one is luxuriously ensconced between sheets, under a thick eiderdown, and the guides rap at the door at one A.M., it is not difficult to imagine the feelings of the condemned, when the entrance of the jailer before daylight admits of only one construction. Then one is inclined to turn over, with a vague sense of injury at the thought of the black cliffs sheathed in ice. But once out in the keen, clear air, well fortified by something hot inside, there comes to the climber a new sense of positive exhilaration at the prospect of the work before him; and the mere fact of being alive is in itself a source of rejoicing. Overhead the sky is cloudless

Raphael Biner on the Last Ice Cornice of the Rothhorn

and star-lit, with a waning moon, not powerful enough to illuminate the depths of shadow thrown across the valley by the heights behind; and for a long distance the path is undistinguishable save in the little circle of light cast by the lantern of the guide in front, so that one is obliged to mind his steps while picking his way from one bowlder to another. In front rises the ragged outline of the Gabelhorn, and the dark masses of rock which conceal the Rothhorn, all in the diffused and spectral light which comes just before dawn.

Once out of the gloom and shadow, the lantern is extinguished; behind us, and beyond the vague darkness which still lurks in the ravine of the Trift, arise the spotless snows of the Monte Rosa chain, cutting sharply against the first pink flush of the sky. Then follows the matchless pageant of early dawn, and the sunrise, which has an impressive solemnity in these high latitudes unequalled elsewhere. More than once I have seen the guides halt in their steps and turn back to enjoy it, accustomed as they are to the spectacle; and it is always a pleasure to see in their rough-hewn, weather-beaten faces the gleam of recognition which shows that they too are keenly alive to its beauty.

Long before this, the last regret at our
enforced early rising has vanished; all
other regrets and cares which may have
followed us to Zermatt have been left behind and forgotten for the moment; most
of them lurk among our belongings left at
the hotel in Zermatt, and not one has
followed us beyond the little room at the
Trift. For the moment the one absorbing
aim in life is to see the end of this inter-
minable moraine. One could not but think
of Dante's obscure wood, —

> " E quanto a dir qual era è cosa dura; "

and beyond the last of the moraine we
mount the ice of the Rothhorn glacier.
There is but little of it; and we come
almost at once to the towering barrier of
rocky precipice at the left, which is the
first formidable outwork of the Rothhorn
itself. Although we could not have been
favored with a milder day for this promenade, the way up the vertical wall, which
lay along the groove worn by a cataract,
was covered with a thin coating of ice,
where the spray had frozen during the
night. The staircase cut by another cas-
cade a little farther on was equally slippery; but after Biner had prospected a
little, he found a way which would con-

duct us to the more gentle slopes above. One of the chief beauties of this particular Rothhorn * is, that it does not give one much leisure for retrospection, but offers in rapid succession almost every variety of climbing necessary to keep one's interest from flagging. When we had gained the summit of the rocks, high above the glacier, we were confronted with a long and exceedingly steep slope of mingled snow and ice, where step-cutting was necessary in places, and one or two halts to gain breath, before we could reach the summit of the long, winding ridge which leads to the peak. Sharp points of rock pierce the snow in some places; but in front of us stretches away, in long perspective, the sharp *arête* which we must traverse, never straight or even, but sinuous, winding, alternately rising and falling, or hanging over in curving cornices, which we must avoid by long détours, so that it seems at times like being on the ridgepole of some vast white cathedral. The snow has begun to melt a little, and it is not difficult to keep one's footing; but in places where the wind, by constant friction, has left only

---

* Near Zermatt alone there are three Rothhorns. The Unter-Rothhorn, 10,190 feet; Ober-Rothhorn, 11,214 feet, guides, 10 francs; Zinal-Rothhorn, 13,855 feet, guides, 80 francs.

a knife-like edge, the concentrated attention which is necessary becomes at last
fatiguing, so that it is with a sense of relief that we descend steeply the end of
the *arête*, and cautiously mount a slender
bridge of snow like a white flying buttress,
supported from below by a spur or thin
curtain of rock which runs out from the
base of the peak.

We are now at the foot of the mighty
pyramid of splintered rock, powdered in
places with fresh snow, which rises in
front to a discouraging height; and we
can realize in a measure that there is
work before us. Moving carefully across
the slope, through loose snow and over
rocks, we reach the steep and narrow *couloir* filled with ice by which we mount to
the "saddle." Here the guides deposit
their sacks and all superfluous articles, and
we fortify ourselves with a third breakfast.
In doing this sort of work, one feels the
need of a substantial banquet at least once
every two hours. The place is a veritable
saddle; for on the other side the slope is
quite as steep, so that it is almost like sitting astride of a wall. Even the piollets
are left behind, with the exception of Biner's, who takes the lead, and does the
cutting. In places like this only a prac-

tised expert can carry his axe without being embarrassed by it, when both hands are needed, and where the best-trained acrobat would be manifestly inferior to a Barbary ape. The thin wedge of rock on which we have been sitting stops at the foot of a wall; there is no difficulty in getting up, as the notches occur in the right places, and one gains a little extra confidence for what is before him. Now comes something quite different,—a broad table-like surface of smooth rock, sloping downward with such a degree of convexity as to hide the base of the mountain below; and beyond its curving edge nothing is visible nearer than the glaciers of the Zinal Valley. Too steep to walk across, and with little or no apparent irregularity of surface, it resembles the smooth, rounded slope of a mansard roof. But a closer inspection discloses two or three transverse fissures; and one by one, with great caution, we manage to wriggle across, eel-like, depending on our fingers, elbows, and the friction of our clothes, but not at all on our feet. It is in reality much easier than it looks, as one feels instinctively where to bestow his weight. Upon the other side, some sharp jutting points of rock afford a safe anchorage,

Getting Down the Ledge above the Saddle — Rothhorn

where we may take breath for a moment, and looking upward contemplate the next bit of work. Although widely different in character, it is not a whit more inviting. A long and glassy ice-slope of exceeding steepness leads straight to the top of the ridge near the first peak; a narrow ledge or ridge of rock begins high up, and, protruding through the ice, reaches about half-way down the slope; to gain this point is the object of the next effort. While Peter and I enjoy the well-earned luxury of indolence, Biner goes on and hacks away with his piollet, cutting a series of deep gashes in the hard ice; half-way to the lower end of the ledge he reaches the end of his coil of rope, and shouts for us to come up. Leaving Peter to await his turn at the bottom, I mount this Jacob's ladder of ice as far as the rope will permit, there to wait until Biner has gained the rocks. To describe this slope as nearly vertical would be to exaggerate; but it certainly has the inclination of the average straight "mansard," and to walk would necessitate too much effort in keeping one's balance. Fortunately the steps are so deep that it is possible to rest an elbow in one, and a knee in another; the blows of the piollet above send down a shower of ice chips which fill up the steps as they are cut, and it becomes necessary to scoop them out with one's fingers. Meanwhile there is leisure to look around and enjoy the landscape. There is a remarkably fine view of the Dent Blanche, which seems to have borrowed very nearly the outline of the Matterhorn when seen from the Staffel Alp; * but most of the scenery is down in the depths beyond and below the placid countenance of Peter, which stands out at the bottom of the ice-slope, against the deep gulf of the Zinal Valley, for the smooth convexity of the slope effectually conceals everything between. Biner reaches the rocks, and we mount rapidly until we can lay hold of the first sharp ridge; at this point two or three slender cords †

---

* See addendum at the end of this article on *The Matterhorn from the Staffel Alp.*

† This extract from the *Alpine Post*, a bright little Swiss journal (Sept. 6, 1893), will show that such improvements do not always meet with the unqualified approval of the public: "One has been accustomed to look on the Dent Blanche as unlikely ever to be degraded by being bound in ropes and chains. But, alas! a party ascending it not long ago found to their intense disgust that a rope had been fixed from the end of the traverse below the first 'Gendarme' to the *arête*. In this country it is illegal to remove anything such as ropes off a mountain, otherwise no doubt the cord would have been cut away then and there. . . . Climbers will remember the piece of ground covered by this rope. Our correspondent, when ascending the Dent Blanche, found this part of the mountain in the worst possible condition; and he does not hesitate to say that for an experienced party (and 'duffers' should not attack first-class peaks) there was no danger whatever, though great care was requisite in cutting the steps."

protrude from the ice. Some one has evidently taken the trouble to fasten them before the ice had formed; but they are hardly strong enough to bear one's weight, and the rocks offer a more secure hold. It is not advisable, however, to attempt walking yet. As the rocks are stratified vertically, they offer no transverse breaks in which to insert one's fingers; but the roughness of their surface is sufficient to allow of a firm hold. A short walk along the crest of the ridge leads us to the first of the two crags which form the summit, and the next step is a gymnastic performance in which some caution is advisable. This first peak runs up into a narrow wedge of rock crowned by thin, pointed slabs like a stone fence, or like gravestones, slanting outward, and over-

Raphael Biner, Guide — Zermatt.

hanging the perpendicular wall on the Zermatt side which seemed so grand and impressive when we looked up at it from the snow *arête* below. Around and under these leaning slabs it is necessary to pass, one by one, placing our feet carefully in a little fissure like the gutter along a house-top, hugging the gravestones which hang over us, and leaning backward until we overhang the abyss, some three thousand feet below. It is easy, however, to shift our hold from one slab to another, and where the fissure ceases there are little projecting points which afford secure footing. And then it is much more agreeable to hang over, back down, than in the reverse sense.

The guide in front, having reached the end of this gallery, suddenly disappears through a gap in the wall, which is like an embrasure between two battlements of a fortress, barely wide enough for us to squeeze through, one by one; the passage descends steeply like a stairway encumbered with snow, and we come out on the Zinal side again. The last peak is just in front of us, but to reach it the way lies across a slender ice-bridge running upward to the peak at a decided angle. The accumulated snow hangs over the cornice in beautiful curves and rounded masses, fringed in places with long icicles, where it caps the wall on the Zermatt side. While Biner goes ahead, and hacks out a passage with his piollet, there is barely time to scrawl a sketch of the situation in front; * and then with a brief scramble up the rocks beyond the cornice, we are on the summit. There is just room for two of us to sit on the same rock, and the third crouches below while we finish the provisions carried in our pockets; for the guides' sacks have been left on the "saddle," and the bulk of the supplies far below. Getting down is an easy matter at first, cautiously descending the cornice, along the gallery, which might be less agreeable on a cold day

---

* For those sketches illustrating climbing episodes, the writer does not claim topographical accuracy; since most of them were materialized from hasty notes, and aim merely to render his own impressions at the moment. The one showing the last snow cornice on the Rothhorn was, however, made from a more careful scrawl; and the main lines were closely followed, as there was an opportunity to do this while the leader was cutting steps. There are many places where a small camera may be used, and there are others where it would be extremely injudicious to allow one's attention to wander from the work in hand; and they are precisely the places where an amateur would want to make a snap-shot. It is no more than fair to consider the guides at such moments; and unless one is a member of the C. A., and presumably *à la hauteur de la situation* (whatever it may be), or is as clever an acrobat as the man at the Folies Bergère, who changes his clothes on a tight rope and breaks moving glass bulbs with a Winchester at the same time, he had better be content with doing one thing well, and to remember that *there is no net under him.*

with a high wind; and we do not forget to exercise a certain amount of calm deliberation when we get to the steep ice-slope. Then comes the sloping rock; and here one cannot but envy the unerring judgment of that "expert" who figures so often in the pages of "Baedeker," and whose presumed superiority is particularly aggravating in the passages marked, "for experts only, with the best guides." It is not so easy to find the projections or fissures as it was in getting up; and about half-way down, when Peter's head had disappeared below the verge, the last crevice seemed to have disappeared also, in the smooth surface of the rock. Hearing the hoarse voice of the guide behind, I look up, and see that he has taken a turn of the rope around a rock, and has braced himself against it; so letting go, I slide down to the bottom, and then down the ledge to the saddle. . . . It was sunset when we reached the glacier, and darkness overtook us before we got to the bottom of the moraines and the Trift valley. A light far below, which we at first mistook for the window of the inn, proved to be the lantern of the hotel-keeper, who had come out to meet us. We had been out over seventeen hours in

all, and the unexpected depth of the snow
must in any case have added several hours
to the usual time. It was our intention
to keep on to Zermatt that night; but
having feasted royally, and quenched our
thirst, no one seemed disposed to carry
out the valiant intentions of an hour ago.
Moreover, we may have remembered at
that moment the sad fate of the German
climber, who, having scaled one of the
giants, was proceeding homeward at night
down an actual path, by lantern-light,
when he stumbled and fell into a gulley
a few feet below, with most unpleasant
results; and we concluded then not to
face the dangers of the path down the
Trift valley before daylight.

v.

Between the guides of Zermatt, Evo-
lena, and other centres of Alpinism in the
Valais, it would be somewhat invidious to
make any distinction; but those whose
portraits are here given have accompanied
the writer on many excursions, and although each one of them has had more
favorable opportunities of showing his
prowess, they are all men whose strength,
endurance, and general capacity are equal

to any emergency. It would be hardly doing fair justice to the reader, as well as to the subject, to show only the bright side of it, and not to make the admission that it has a seamy side as well. With the yearly increase of travel, many charming excursions which were easy to make a few years ago, are becoming more difficult, — the hap-hazard wandering with a knap-sack from one valley to another, when one was always sure of finding a bed some-where. In the Tyrol, for instance, where comfortable hotels are rarer, the pedestrian had better take along a shelter-tent and proceed on an independent basis. It was the writer's experience this last season to enter the valley of Sulden (near Meran) over a high pass where both he and the guide were well drenched by a sudden storm of rain and sleet; and upon arrival in the village they were unable to find sleeping accommodations, or even a place to change their clothing, the few cabarets which did duty as hotels being crammed with German and Austrian tourists. When one has only a brief space of time, a fort-night or three weeks, to spend among the giants, he may as well make up his mind to take what comes in his way, and not to set his heart upon any particular one, least

A Rest on the Way Down

of all on the uncertain and capricious Dent
Blanche, and to have some other alternative,
some other seductive programme in view,
by way of compensation, should he chance
upon a season of bad weather. When one
is fairly penned up and snow-bound in some
high and desolate valley, there is nothing
for him to do but watch the dance of the
merry snow-flakes through the window-
panes, in the privacy of his own quarters,
where the pattern of the wall-paper, should
there be any, is often exasperating to his
vexed spirit, and afflicts him as an additional grievance if he is at all susceptible
to harmony of color; or he may hang over
the stove in the common room, wrapped
in an ulster, and try to find oblivion in the
pages of the "London, Chatham, & Dover
Railway Guide," or hunt for the missing
pages of the "pension novel."   It is then
that he will think of Pallanza, where the
summer still lingers, of long pulls on the
lake, and breakfast in the vine-roofed por-
tico of some little albergo on the shore —
of Venice, and the swimmers at the Lido
— and if he does not care to retrace his
steps back to the starting-point, he will
find a porter to carry his bag over one or
two of the minor passes, where fresh snow
has covered the green pasture slopes and has

drifted neck-deep on the cols; and thence down to the Valley of Gressonny or the Val Sesia, and so on to the chestnut-woods and the sunshine.

———

An ascent of the Matterhorn, made some time after the foregoing article was printed, has elicited from the author the following addendum : ——

The outline of the Matterhorn from the Staffel Alp, or indeed from almost any point of view, is a striking instance of optical illusion. The north *arête*, by which it is usually ascended from the Zermatt side, appears to mount almost vertically to the great bulging shoulder near the summit, and to study its ragged edge and giddy windings from below has a rather disheartening effect on the timid amateur. It is only when seen in profile, or when one is actually on it, that its terrors are sensibly diminished ; and instead of working his way up the angle of a tower, the climber has to surmount a series of rocky pinnacles, which might be likened to the ruins of a score of Gothic cathedrals. Were the ropes and chains removed from the cone, it would again become the most dangerous and uncertain of peaks ; for al-

though other ascents may present more
difficult problems in climbing, there are
few summits which afford so slight a foothold, so little to take hold of, and where
one is more at the mercy of the elements
and the unforeseen. And there are few
which consist entirely of peak, without the
tedious prelude of moraine and glacier, and
endless slopes of *névé*, where the real work
begins at the very outset, when one leaves
the *cabane*. But oh, the grandeur of it
all! This working one's way by lantern-
light along the face of a wall which seems
to tower upward to the stars, where the
sloping glacier below might lie at any
depth — ten, fifty, or a thousand feet.
There is a good bit of glacier work
which comes in, if I remember rightly,
on the way down. The angle of the descent is here so violent that it is not unlike
getting down a half-frozen drift lying on
a steep roof, although the base of the cliff
on the left affords secure handhold. A
feature which adds much to the apparent
height and majesty of the Matterhorn is
the almost vertical downward trend or
plunge of all the lines which radiate from
the apex, whether couloirs, ravines, crevasses, or the slope of the snow-fields, the
very stratification and fractures of the rock,

and indeed all the vast complexity of details which go to make up its architecture.

This mountain, of all others, seems to be regarded with more respect by the Gaul than by his Anglo-Saxon neighbors across the Channel. He has at the same time more vague and uncertain notions of its history. On the first page of one of the leading Parisian dailies, there was a surprising announcement last season, to the effect that "the terrible Mount Cervin" had actually been ascended for the first time in many years,—and by an American. It had, however, been conquered at some remote date by two Frenchmen. The editor must have received a shower of ironical comments from the brotherhood of climbers, telling him of the caravans of tourists which now swarm up its sides every fine day in the season; for the very next morning there was an elaborate attempt to remove the false impression which was due to a printer's error. It should have read, "ascended for the first time this season." But the correction was hardly adequate to explain away the general impression left by the paragraph.

AN ASCENT

OF MOUNT ÆTNA

By A. F. Jaccaci

Illustrated by the author.

In the Lava of 1886.

RAVELLING away from Paris in the late autumn days, there passes gradually out of my vision the gray landscape of France, filled with melancholy signs of the decline and decay of nature. As the train leaves the Alps behind, and descends toward Turin, the charm of the south begins to make itself felt. With each succeeding hour it grows in witchery,—a brightness, a warm

129

radiance that rejuvenates mind and body, and sets one's whole being on the alert to enjoy every feature of the new scenes.

The trip from Paris to Sicily in this season, from fields strewn with sere leaves, powdered with hoar-frost, and lined by desolate trees stretching their naked branches in dumb entreaty, to the breathing, expansive nature of Italy, acts on the senses as a powerful stimulant. One drinks pleasure with each look cast at sky and sea of such deep, iridescent color; at landscapes garbed in abundant vegetation, and spotted with villages set in the shadows of ancient castles; at chains of hills looking in the distance like trembling veils of light. The fatigue and tedium of a sixty hours' trip are easily forgotten in the succession of fresh sensations.

Taormina, midway between Messina and Catania, is my first resting-place; and after a night's sleep in a bed 'tis good to wake breathing the sweet-scented mountain air that vibrates with echoing guttural cries of street-venders and tinkling of church-bells. Bright sunlight floods my room, and through the open window little houses, all white amid the foliage, look like an alighting of doves in a garden. Beyond are rows of mountains; some near,

all rugged; the
farthest, sugges-
tions more than
realities.

From a ter-
race I look
down a pre-
cipitous in-
cline four hundred
feet deep on the scattered
huts of a fishing village.
An immense stretch of
coast juts out its prom-
ontories and curves its
bays from that village
to the far distant hori-
zon; and between the

Women of Nicolosi.

blue and the green of sea and land, the
sandy shore seems a golden ribbon, growing narrow till it is lost in haze.

Fitly crowning the tableau is the goal
of my trip, Ætna, rising gently from the
sea until its head towers above all else. I
had first seen, from a car window as the
train crawled along the southern coast of
Calabria, this giant guardian of the flock
of hills which constitute the island of
Sicily; and from near as from far it brings
to one's mind the striking epithets be-
stowed on it by Pindar, " Father of the

Clouds," " Pillar of Heaven." Ever covered with clouds, so that its immutable mass of rock, and the airy, fanciful shapes, uniting in endless combinations their dual natures, appear as a composite whole, Ætna is indeed of earth and heaven. The shining sun glorifies it, the moving shadows of its crown of cloud-banks give to it an always changing aspect, and through the clear atmosphere appears distinctly its furrowed garment of craters and valleys, lava torrents, and forests.

In this marvellous panorama, facing which the ancient Greeks, with their passionate feeling for beauty, had placed the theatre of Taormina, one does not realize the colossal bulk of the volcano. The range of vision is such that the component parts, simple details in a grandiose *ensemble*, lose their individual value. Yet from eastern to western spur Ætna covers forty miles, and more than forty towns and villages are strung in rosaries of bright beads over its flanks and feet.

From the highest rows of seats in the Greek theatre, with the ruined stage as foreground, there unfolds that panorama like the most sublime of backgrounds. From down the stage, framed in superbly by broken columns and fragments of brick

On the Road to Nicolosi

walls, Ætna's solitary cone, set against the
southern sky, is a symphony of snow and
azure, of mother-of-pearl whites and transparent blues—an ineffably soft and vaporous vision.

On the way to Catania, shortly after
leaving Taormina, the train passes through
several tunnels cut in ranges of lava. The
first savage marks of the volcano are these
torrents of solid matter that from the central mass twenty miles away have run into
the sea, forming continuous ridges. A few
miles beyond them one enters fully into
Ætna's kingdom. There against an uni-
formly purplish background,—the purple
of lava,—springs forth the brilliant leaf-
age of orange, lemon, and fig trees, and of
vines, chastened by the silvery sheen of the
classical olive. White splashes in this bubbling color, where all the gamuts of greens
and purples mix and melt, are the walls of
tiny houses quaintly built, and to the hur-
ried passer-by mysteriously suggestive of
the character of their unseen inmates.

It is a sight of singular beauty, this
earth, which is but lava ground to dust,
so enveloped in the tenderness of growing
vegetation. The patience and industry of
generations of men have changed the once
grim wastes into things of loveliness. Yet

A View of Mount Ætna from the Greek Theatre at Taormina.

now and again the nether monster reveals
his power. Like marks of the lion's paw
are seen lonely cairns of the frothing,
seething matter stopped in mid rush, and
turned to stone. How strange and un-
canny a substance is this lava belched forth
in lightnings and thunder from a mountain in labor, — a sooty mineral calcinated
to the core; all good substance in it destroyed, leaving but a skeleton embryo
scorched and shapeless, that gives an awful impression of the agonies of its birth
and death !

The train in skirting but the western side of the volcano rambles incessantly through tunnels and by embankments of lava. From the fact that the other sides bear no less testimony to frequent devastations, one gathers an idea of the extent of those eruptions, whose unbroken record is carried down from prehistoric times to our day.

The average of eruptions in this century alone is one every four or five years. Fortunately Ætna has had long periods of rest following its active moods. Noticing that these periods alternate with those of Vesuvius, scientists have inferred that there is a subterranean connection between the two, and that they belong to a group of which the Lipari Islands are a minor part, and the little island of Pantelleria the last outlying summit.

All poets of antiquity were familiar with Ætna. Curiously enough, Homer does not allude to its volcanic character except in his episode of the blinded Cyclops, Polyphemus, hurling rocks after Ulysses, which is but a transparent myth of the molten lava rolling down the mountain with such impetus as to leap from the high cliffs far out into the sea, forming those islets still known to the Sicilians as the seven "*Scoglie dei Ciclopi.*" The war of the Titans against Jupiter, the forge of Vulcan, allude, no doubt, to eruptive phenomena utterly inexplicable, that by their very suddenness and magnitude seemed not less than supernatural to the pantheistic imagination of the Greeks.

The Church of Trecca, with Lava-stone Decoration.

Ætna, placed in Magna Grecia, the oldest historical ground of Europe, and at the doors of Athens and Rome, has been visited and described by many eminent personages of classic antiquity, — Pindar, who narrates the eruption of B.C. 476;

Aristotle that of B.C. 340 ; Pythagoras, Sappho, Thucydides ; Empedocles, who found a voluntary death in its crater ; Cicero, Catullus, Virgil, Ovid, Diodorus, Strabo, Suetonius, etc. ; and through them even the memory of a violent outbreak in prehistoric times, that made the Sicanians abandon the district, has come down to us.

To look from a speeding train, the embodiment of the tendencies and achievements of our epoch, at that landscape, teeming with the souvenirs of generations whose ashes are mingled with the ashes of the volcano, stirs the mind to a train of philosophic thought. How can we help feeling the pathos of that history of the life-and-death struggles of twenty-five hundred years come home to each of us, when we are so forcibly reminded of the fragility of human effort and life before that nature, ever living, ever young, ever cruelly indifferent to the passing human herd ?

From its huge neighbor Catania borrows the chief objects of its adornment. Blocks of volcanic material are used for the pavement of streets, the construction of houses, and often also in the exterior decoration of important buildings. The idea

Mount Ætna

of relieving the white stone façades with
ornamental details wrought in dark lava,
when judiciously carried out, is well
adapted to the curious style of architecture known as Sicilian, a composite of three
distinct styles, — the Byzantine, Arab, and
Norman.

Despite its originality, its cleanliness, the
city to me has a stinted, formal look, un-
picturesque in the extreme; but it may be
that the far from good name Catania bears
in Italy, a name synonymous with unfair
dealing, prejudices me. It is a fact that
reckless speculation, characterized by a
deluge of worthless promissory notes, has
within a few years plunged the once flour-
ishing Catania into a most miserable condition. Not having visited it since the
days of its boom, I was struck by one pleasant evidence of the usefulness of worldly
misfortune, which had transformed the
boom-period dummies attired in ultra-
gaudy finery into sensible folk, oblivious
to the etiquette of Italian city manners
and who wore their old clothes, and had
worn them so long that shiny seams and
scrupulous patches bespoke a poverty sin-
cere as it was self-respecting.

I had to journey toward Nicolosi, my
starting-point for the ascent of Ætna, be-

hind one of those thin, unfortunate brutes, a Catanian horse; not, however, without making an express bargain that under no condition should the whip be used. "Ma, signor!" the driver had exclaimed in amazement; "he won't go!" Well, he did go, but very gently, for the drive is a hard twelve miles of steady up-hill grade.

The road winds and clambers pleasantly between vine-hung walls and peeping villas. The little retaining stone walls incasing each field on the rapid slopes are almost buried in verdure; umbrella pines look down from their loftiness, and once in a while some dead crater protrudes its burnt head above the sea of living things.

It is vine harvest. Files of burdened donkeys pass us, prodded on by the peasants following with swift and swinging strides. These *contadini* stare at us intently, yet with faces immobile, and so brown and furrowed, so sharp of contour, that they might have been cut from the dark soil beneath. Miserable beyond belief, submissive in suffering, they have the dull gaze of ruminants, the soul asleep, the mind alert only for food and shelter; and their types, bearing the stamp of their great ancestors, the Greeks, somewhat mixed with traits of former alien oppressors,—

Ætna from the Harbor of Catania.

Arabs, Normans, Spaniards, — are the living witnesses in our day of the glory and vicissitudes of their race through the ages.

Night falls as I reach Nicolosi and its primitive inn, deserted now, as it is past the season for climbing the mountain.

The chief of the Guides of Ætna, a corporation established by the Catania branch of the Alpine Club, comes to make the necessary arrangements for my trip. At six the next morning the guide arrives, straps the provisions on his back, and we are off.

The road, threading vineyards, is flanked a few hundred feet to our left by a serrated fin, standing a defiant barricade before two big reddish cones, the Monte Rossi, upheaved in 1669 by an eruption which almost destroyed Catania. Scarcely a mile from the village we came to the limit of the lava of 1886, which, pouring in a vast flood down the slopes, seemed about to sweep away the Altarelli, an open chapel dedicated to the three patron saints of Nicolosi. The priests, with a piety no doubt strengthened by terror, displayed the veil of Santa Agata, a holy relic which in Catania has performed miracles innumerable; and the destructive lava, respecting the sanctuary, divided in two branches, leaving it untouched.

It would have been a personal insult to my guide, who proudly related this story, to notice that the Altarelli is built on an eminence, and that there is present evidence that when the fiery stream reached this point, it must have been in its last spasms, for a few feet beyond it stopped altogether. Besides, it would have been a useless task; as every good Nicolosian considers a natural explanation of the miraculous event an invention of the devils, enemies of his patron saints.

View from Monte Gemellari, showing some of the Mouths of the Eruption of 1886.

Any way, I was soon too busy to think of miracles. A mule-path skirts the lava-bed of 1886, but the quickest route lies straight across it. We took this short cut; and it gave me a full taste of volcano climbing, to the understanding of which a few words of explanation are necessary.

Liquid lava has two distinct forms: the first, when, issuing in a bubbling mass, it flows like compact gruel; the second,

when in the subterranean depths water
coming in temporary contact with burning liquids, the two elements issue pell-
mell. The imprisoned steam, tearing and
bellowing within the molten lava, whose
temperature often exceeds 2,000° Fahren-
heit, bursts forth, hurling to the heavens
fiery, chaotic masses. Continuous explo-
sions upheave the masses again and again
into air, pounding and grinding them
against one another. Thus they leap and
fall, battering and battered, in Titanic,
vertiginous dance, scattering, as from a
monstrous engine of destruction, a storm-
rain of rocks, sand, and ashes. Now, imagine this inferno caught in its maddest,
wildest activity, and held fast, the knife-
edge excrescences bristling all over it like
savage teeth gnawing the air, the awful
piling up on its heaving sides of the very
vitals of the volcano, and you will have an
idea of this lava which for seventeen days
of the spring of 1886 furrowed and deso-
lated a thousand acres of fair country into
semblance of hell.*

We descend into valleys and pits, silent

* The new crater of the Monte Gemellari, situated four and
a half miles above Nicolosi, at an altitude of four thousand six
hundred and fifty feet, was formed May 19, 1886, after a violent
earthquake. Lava flowed until June 3, reaching within half a
mile of Nicolosi.

and dusky as the portals to the world of
the dead, whose monochrome dark purplish tone makes their aspect more sinister.
The forbidding stones rise in ragged walls
piled into fantastic shapes, and rivers of
rigid lava writhe serpent-like about this
Laocoön of Ætna.

It is a severe test of endurance to force
our way for a long hour and a half across
these diabolical wastes, every
instant looking down to
find the next foothold, and
jumping from stone to
stone, tottering, falling,

The Little Path Threading the Vineyards on the Slopes of Ætna.

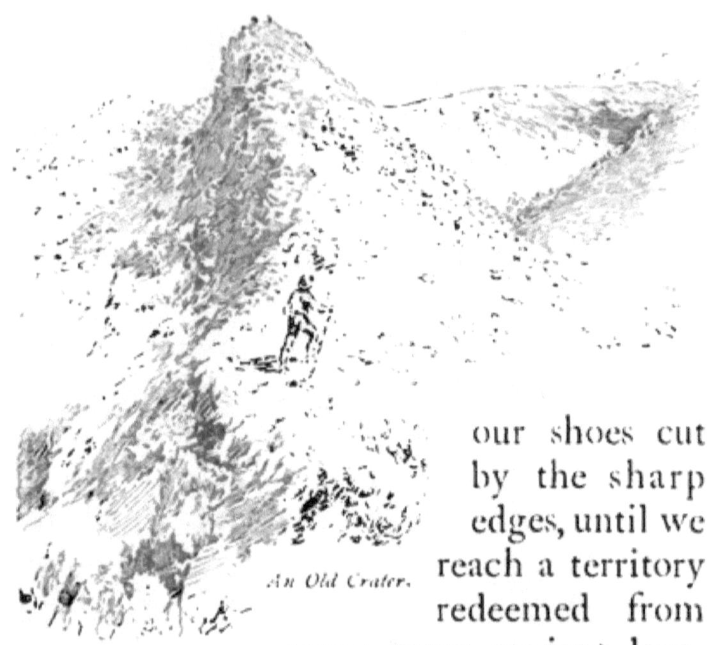

An Old Crater.

our shoes cut by the sharp edges, until we reach a territory redeemed from some more ancient lava-bed, as this desert will also be redeemed in a century or two.

Amid the vineyards, along a little path hemmed in by stone walls, *contadini* meet and pass us. Here asperities have been somewhat smoothed down by constant travel, the rougher, larger stones removed, the gaping holes filled. Time and nature have spread a surface soil, where flourish wild plants starred with fragile blossoms.

We pass near craters, of which a continuous array will precede us to the highest cone ; yet we see but a very small part of the mountain, whose craters extend on every side within a radius of twenty miles.

Thinking of what terrible conflagrations, loss of life and property, these are proof of, the power within appears extraordinarily formidable.

Now the stately mountain seems to rise in its might above and over our heads, though its crest is hidden in cloud. The vegetation about lacks the orange and lemon trees; we have passed their altitude. Sturdy vines continue the fight longer, but we leave them also behind. Big oaks and chestnuts, copper beeches, birches, and the tall Laricio pines, keep us company till we arrive, four hours from Nicolosi, at the way-house in the woods,—*Casa del Bosco*, 4,215 feet above the sea-level. We are higher than the summit of Vesuvius; the air has grown perceptibly sharper, and is now quite cold.

After lunch and a rest, having taken in a supply of water for the remainder of the journey, we resume climbing through a narrow and crooked valley, along a zigzag path barely discernible in the chaotic confusion. The higher we reach, the more pleasant it is to turn and look back on the constantly growing panorama of bleak volcanic stretches dotted with woods and gaping cavities; farther below, floating in the green, are villages,—Catania, then the

On the Brink of the Great Crater of Ætna.

turquoise sea, and far out the hilly coast terminated by Cape Augusta, behind which Syracusa hides. Here and there isolated clusters of birches and pines, set in an undergrowth of gigantic ferns, mark all that remains of the dense forests which, as late as the last century, entirely covered Ætna's flanks. These trees no longer soften the stern impression of our surroundings. In a rarified atmosphere that dwarfs and stunts them, they lose all beauty, and simply vegetate between life and death. Becoming rare, they disappear entirely as we enter the *"Regione Deserta,"* the region of cold and death, where the nakedness of rock is absolutely unrelieved. A bright sun imparts neither cheer nor warmth, but, striking the velvety darkness of the lava, gives it a steely, glittering aspect, as though the mountain were clad in chain-armor.

The wind rises and falls; blustering gusts in the couloirs and on the plateaus are succeeded by delightful lulls. Mists, thin as veils, and threatening storm-clouds, drift slowly and softly, rolling, lifting, and revealing vistas of bleak mounds piled high. This quiet, delicate life, playing in goblin-like fashion about these rigid and desolate scenes, is inexpressibly lovely. Such sights and sensations charm the long hours of an ascent, arduous and intensely fatiguing, though devoid of the worse dangers and consequent excitement of Alpine climbing.

The trail becomes steeper and steeper as we catch a first glimpse of the deservedly called "*Serra del Solfizio*," a saw-shaped ridge, whose feet are sunk in enormous hollows filled with eternal snow. This is our first sign of the neighborhood of the magnificent Valle del Bove, reached after crossing a tableland, — the Piano del Lago. We skirt the edge of the cliffs, three thousand feet deep, which form a border on all its sides, except for an open gap toward the east.

Geologically, this basin, three miles in width, is the most interesting part of Ætna, as competent authorities unite in considering it the original crater. On its brink stands the Tower of the Philosopher, presumably the ruin of an observatory built for the Emperor Hadrian on the occasion of his visit to the volcano.

I am too thoroughly exhausted to do justice to any more sights; and it is with the yearning of the flesh that at last I see at the base of the central cone two white buildings, — the Observatory and a refuge, both unoccupied at present. We have the key to the latter, the Casa Inglesi; so called because it was built by English officers during the English occupation of Sicily in Napoleonic times. Though rebuilt and enlarged by the Alpine Club of Catania, it remains a primitive affair, its walls lined with bunks, one above another, as in a ship's steerage; yet it affords welcome shelter against a cold so intense that our beards and coats are united in a covering of ice.

Too tired to talk, we sup hastily, and fall asleep in utter weariness, our bodies sunk in yielding straw, our feet to the fire, which warms, soothes, relaxes the strained muscles, and sets the blood to buzzing the most effective of lullabys.

Awakening at midnight, I leave the guide to gather up himself and our traps while I go outside. The door closes behind me, and I stand alone in the night.

The Serra del Solfizio, from the Valle del Bove.

Lo! what a strange stillness there is in this outer world. The wind, blowing fitfully, is charged with unearthly smells and faint echoes of subterranean seethings and rumblings. From invisible holes snaky vapors rise and quiver in spiral contortions.

Monstrous shapes of lava, like Titanic dead upon a battlefield, lie on the plateau; their icy profiles, brought out by the oblique rays of a waning moon, shine weirdly among inky shadows, until these threatening rocks seem the gathering of a silent demoniac host to overwhelm and ingulf us. But the guide opens the refuge door, and at the light of his lantern the phantasmagoria vanishes.

I take my axe; and we start to pick our way, among treacherous crevices, yawning and bottomless, toward the crater that lifts above us its twelve hundred feet of immaculate whiteness.

In August an ascent of the last cone, whose perfectly smooth sides slide down at a gradient of thirty-five degrees, is comparatively easy because of the absence of snow; but thus late in the autumn the thick snow, hardened into ice, and nightly covered with fresh coats, compels the frequent cutting of steps. That means hard work and dangerous. It takes two hours to reach the brink of the crater, a single abyss two or three miles in circumference, from whose depths emerge countless wreaths of thin, damp smoke. The impression of that silent gulf, with its vitality expressed only by the sulphurous, nauseat-

Peasants by the Way.

ing vapors incessantly rising, curling, and disappearing, is supremely grand. Beside Ætna, one remembers Vesuvius's sputterings as the efforts of an infant.

It was three o'clock when I stood, eleven thousand feet above the sea-level, on a small pyramid of ashes which keeps guard over the crater and the whole of Ætna. The north wind having cleared the atmosphere, brushing away clouds and haze, all circumstances were favorable to my watching the sun rise.

The moon has now disappeared, leaving no trace of her passage. Sky, sea, and land are of the same color, an immensity of indistinct blue, clearer somewhat overhead, darker around and below. The only sensation of being at a great height is the piercing cold that keeps us moving about, stamping our feet on the ice, that resounds sonorously, as if it were but a thin covering over cavernous depths. A change of color, so gradual that it is more felt than seen, begins. A subdued radiance, opal, dissolving into a suggestion of pink, tinges the east. The details of the crater become more distinct as night recedes to the lowlands. Impalpable grayish light creeps up, invading the heavens, and Aurora's rosy refulgence increases every moment— a veiled splendor, a symphony *en sourdine* of exquisitely delicate tints, restful and lovely. A like scene must have suggested the poet's descriptions of the Elysian Fields.

Banks of billowy clouds wall up that part of the horizon where the sun is to appear. Their fleecy bosoms rise and swell, yield and part, before the oncoming dawn.

Above them the glory of light continues to grow. I keep my eyes anxiously strained on the most luminous spot, whence of a sudden a dart of light crosses space, fleeting over the sea. That dart increases into a golden streak, clearly cut, for a perceptible moment, on the purplish water. It changes to a flood of light while the disk of the sun emerges slowly from under the horizon. The shadows palpitate, dissolve

about the crest of Ætna, transfiguring her
into an island of gold and rose. Passionate-
ly now the day advances, flinging wide her
magic skirts. The lower valleys awake, the
colors of their vegetation glow and dance.
The trees lift up their heads; it seems as
if in that profound stillness one could hear
the murmur of the reanimation of things.
The sun touches every corner of his vast
kingdom; day — full day — is with us.

Beautiful with the beauty of dreams is
the spectacle.

To the north the archipelago of the
Lipari Islands, with their smoky light-
house of Stromboli, floats on the iridescent sea. To the south, on the border of
the vast horizon, hover two ghosts, Malta
and Pantelleria; while the purple shadows
of the Calabrian Mountains on the main-
land bridge the Straits of Messina, hiding
Charybdis and Scylla. Cameo-cut against
the sea, Sicily lies at our feet, displaying
her fifty towns, her countless villages, the
silver ribbons of her rivers, the thousand
varied details of her uneven soil; and
across her whole length, as a tangible
sign of his dominion, Lord Ætna stretches
his enormous triangular shadow.

THE ASCENT
OF MOUNT ARARAT

By H. F. B. Lynch

Mount Ararat from Erivan, Thirty-five Miles Distant.

PREFATORY NOTE.

THE ascent of Ararat, completed on Sept. 19, 1893, formed an incident in a journey, extending for a period of seven months, which I undertook in 1893–1894 for the purpose of acquiring a better knowledge of the country comprised in a general manner by the limits of the Armenian plateau. I was accompanied during the earlier part of this journey by my cousin, Major H. B. Lynch, of the Dorsetshire Regiment; he was unfortunately obliged to leave me and rejoin his regiment almost immediately after the accomplishment of the ascent. In offering some account of our experiences upon the mountain, it is perhaps only fair to myself to observe that the narrative, whatever other shortcomings of a more essential nature it may possess, has undoubtedly suffered as a presentation and description of great natural objects, which it is no small part of the duty of a writer on such a subject to endeavor adequately to portray, owing to the necessary limits which the space at my disposal has imposed upon its length. Although it is impossible to make up for this deficiency in the course of a brief note, yet I would ask the reader, before actually starting from Aralykh, to equip himself with the following elementary facts and considerations in connection with the country which surrounds Ararat, and with the mountain itself.

Ararat rises from the table-land of Armenia, between the Black and Caspian Seas, in the country comprised within a triangle between the Lakes of Sevanga, Urumia, and Van. At the eastern extremity of the long and narrow range which is known in the country under the general name of Aghri Dagh, and which it is convenient to call the Ararat *system*, — a range which, starting from the neighborhood of the forty-second degree of longitude, bisects the plateau from west to east,—there has been reared by volcanic agency a vast mountain fabric surrounded by plain land on all sides but the western, and on that side joined to this Ararat system by a pass of about seven thousand feet. The Ararat system and the fabric of Ararat compose the southerly wall of the vast plain of the Araxes, a plain which, in the neighborhood of the mountain, has an elevation of about two thousand seven hundred feet. This valley of the Araxes is in many respects remarkable. In the first place, it sinks far below the level of the great table-land of Armenia, to which it belongs, a plateau the higher regions of which are situated at an elevation of about seven thousand feet. Secondly, it is a valley of vast extent, offering immense prospects over a treeless volcanic country, and bounded at great intervals of space by mountains of the most imposing dimensions and appearance. Lastly, it constitutes an open highway from the countries about and beyond the Caspian to the shores of the Euxine and Mediterranean Seas. The northern border of this valley, like the southern, is composed of a single mountain and a mountain system. The line which is begun on the west by the colossal mountain mass of Alagöz is continued toward the east by the chains on the south of Lake Sevanga. This correspondence in the disposition of the mountains on either border is varied by a striking diversity in the forms, — the Ararat system, which faces Alagöz, is distinguished by jagged peaks, dark valleys, and abrupt sides; the Sevanga ranges, on the other hand, which you overlook from the slopes of Ararat, present an outline which is fretted by the shapes of cones and craters, and are flanked by convex buttresses of sand. Both Alagöz and Ararat have been raised by volcanic agency; but while the giant on the north has all the clumsiness of a Cyclops, his brother on the south would seem to personify the union of symmetry with size and grace with strength. I must refrain from pursuing this train of thought farther, content if the hints which it may have opened reveal the great scale upon which nature has worked. A few measurements may lend reality to this somewhat misty conception, and serve to fix our ideas. The pile of Alagöz, rising on the left bank of the Araxes, attains an elevation of 13,436 feet: the length of the mass may be placed at about thirty-five miles; its breadth is about twenty-five. The distance across the valley from the middle slopes of

The Party en route.

Ararat to the summit of Alagöz is no less than fifty-four miles; and from the same point to the first spurs of the Sevanga ranges, about twenty miles. Such are the immediate neighbors of Ararat, and such is the extent of open country spread like a kingdom at his feet.

The fabric of Ararat, composed of two mountains supported by a common base, gathers on the right bank of the river, immediately from the floor of the plain. The plain has at this point an elevation of about two thousand seven hundred feet. The pass which joins this fabric to the Ararat system, to the range which it continues, is situated at the back of the fabric, behind the long northwestern slope: the fabric itself stands out boldly and alone in advance of the satellite chain. The axis, or direction of the length, of the whole fabric is from northwest to southeast; and it is the whole length of the mountain which you see from the valley of the Araxes. It may be helpful to analyze in the briefest manner the outline which there faces you. Far away on your right, in the western distance, a continuous slope rises from a low cape or rocky promontory, which emerges from the even surface of the plain like a coast seen from the sea. The length of this slope has been given by Parrot at no less than twenty miles; and its gradient, even where it rises more perceptibly toward the great dome, is only about eighteen degrees. This northwestern slope reaches the region of perpetual snow at a height of about thirteen thousand five hundred feet, and culminates in the summit of Great Ararat, which immediately faces you, and which has an elevation of 17,916 feet. Although it yields in height to the peaks of the Caucasus in the north, and to Demavend (19,400 feet) in the east, nearly five hundred miles away, yet, as Bryce in his admirable book has observed, there can be but few other places in the world where a mountain so lofty rises from a plain so low. The summit of Great Ararat has the form of a dome, and is covered with perpetual snow. This dome crowns an oval figure, the length of which is from northwest to southeast ; and it is therefore the long side of this dome which you see from the valley of the Araxes. On the southeast, as you follow the outline farther, the slope falls at a more rapid gradient of from thirty to thirty-five degrees, and ends in the saddle between the two mountains at a height of nearly nine thousand feet. From that

*The Dome of Ararat as seen above Sardar-Bulakh
at a height of about 9,000 feet*

point it is the shape of the Little Ararat which continues the outline toward the east; it rises in the shape of a graceful pyramid to the height of 12,840 feet, and its summit is distant from that of Great Ararat a space of nearly seven miles. The southeastern slope of the Lesser Ararat corresponds to the northwestern slope of the greater mountain, and descends to the floor of the river valley in a long and regular train. The unity of the whole fabric, the intimate correspondence of the parts between themselves; in a word, the architectural qualities of this natural work, at once impress the eye, and continue to provide an inexhaustible fund of study, however long may be the period of your stay.

Although the mountain is due to volcanic agency, yet the fires have not been seen during the historical period. A glance at the photographs will show that the surface presents all the characteristics of a very ancient volcano. On the northeastern side, in full view of the Araxes valley, the very heart of Ararat has been exposed by the great earthquake of 1840 following former landslips; a broad cleft extends from base to summit, and is known as the chasm of Arguri.

The fame of having been the first to

scale Ararat belongs to the Russian traveller Parrot, who made the ascent in 1829.
Since that time the number of successful
ascents has been, so far as I have been able
to determine, fourteen, including our own.
Of this total of fifteen the credit of eight
belongs to Russia, while five fall to England, one to Germany, and one to the
United States of America.   H. F. B. L.

THE sun had already risen as I let myself
down through the open casement of the
window and dropped into the garden among
the dry brushwood encumbering its sandy
floor.   Not a soul was stirring, and not a
sound disturbed the composure of an Eastern morning, the great world fulfilling its
task in silence, and all nature sedate and
serene.   A narrow strip of plantation runs
at the back of Aralykh, on the south, sustained by ducts from the Kara Su or Black-
water, a stream which leads a portion of the
waters of the Araxes into the cotton-fields
and marshes which border the right bank.
Within this fringe of slim poplars, and
just on its southern verge, there is a little
mound and an open summer-house, — as
pleasant a place as it is possible to imagine,
but which, perhaps, only differs from other

summer-houses in the remarkable situation which it occupies, and in the wonderful view which it commands. It is placed on the extreme foot of Ararat, exactly on the line where all inclination ceases and the floor of the plain begins. It immediately faces the summit of the larger mountain, bearing about southwest. Before you the long outline of the Ararat fabric fills the southern horizon; the gentle undulations of the northwestern slope, as it gathers from its lengthy train; the bold bastions of the snow-fields rising to the rounded dome; and, farther east, beyond the saddle, where the two mountains commingle, the needle form of the Lesser Ararat, free at this season from snow. Yet, although Aralykh lies at the flank of Ararat, confronting the side which mounts most directly from the plain to the roof of snow, the distance from a perpendicular line drawn through the summit is over sixteen miles. Throughout that space the fabric is always rising toward the snowbank fourteen thousand feet above our heads, with a symmetry, and, so to speak, with a rhythm of structure, which holds the eye in spell. First, there is a belt of loose sand, about two miles in depth, beginning on the margin of marsh and irrigation, and seen from this garden, which

The Summit, Viewed from a Height of 13,000 Feet.

directly aligns it, like the sea-bed from a grove on the shore. On the ground of yellow thus presented rests a light tissue of green, consisting of the sparse bushes of the ever-fresh camelthorn, a plant which strikes down into beds of moisture deep-seated beneath the surface of the soil. Although it is possible, crossing this sand-zone, to detect the growing slope, yet this feature is scarcely perceptible from Ara-lykh, whence its smooth, unbroken surface and cool relief of green suggest the appear-ance of an embroidered carpet spread at the threshhold of an Eastern temple for the services of prayer. Beyond this band or belt of sandy ground, composed, no doubt, of a pulverized detritus which the piety of Parrot was quick to recognize as a leaving of the Flood, the broad and massive base of Ararat sensibly gathers and inclines, seared by the sinuous furrows of dry watercourses, and stretching, uninterrupted by any step or obstacle, hill or terrace or bank, to the veil of thin mist which hangs at this hour along the higher seams. Not a patch of verdure, not a streak of brighter color, breaks the long monotony of ochre in the burnt grass and the bleached stones. All the subtle sensations with which the living earth surrounds us — wide as are the tracts of barren desert within the limits of the plain itself — seem to stop arrested at the fringe of this plantation, as on a magician's line. When the vapors obscuring the middle slopes of the mountain dissolve and disappear, you see the shadowed jaws of the great chasm, — the whole side of the mountain burst asunder, from the cornice of the snow-roof to the base, the base itself depressed and hollow throughout its width of about ten miles. No cloud has yet climbed to the snows of the summit shining in the brilliant blue.

It was the morning of the 17th of September, a period of the year when the heat has moderated; when the early air, even in the plain of the Araxes, has acquired a suggestion of crispness, and the sun still overpowers the first symptoms of winter chills.* The tedious arrangements of Eastern travel occupied the forenoon; and it had been arranged that we should dine with our host, the lieutenant, before making the final start. Six little hacks, impressed in the district, and sadly wanting in flesh, were loaded with our effects; our party was mounted on Cossack horses, which, by the extreme courtesy of the Russian authorities, had been placed at our disposal for a week. We took leave of our new friend under a strong sentiment of gratitude and esteem; but a new and pleasurable surprise was awaiting us as we passed down the neat square. All the Cossacks at that time quartered in Aralykh — the greater number were absent on the slopes of the mountain, serving the usual patrols — had been drawn up in marching order, awaiting the arrival of their colonel, who had contrived to keep the secret by expressing his willingness to accompany us a few versts of the way. My cousin and I were

* At Aralykh the thermometer ranged between 60° and 70° F. between the hours of six A.M. and nine A.M. on the several mornings. At mid-day it rose to about 80°.

The Great Chasm of Arguri.

riding with the colonel, and the purpose of
these elaborate arrangements was explained
to us with a sly smile: the troop, with their
colonel, were to escort us on our first day's
journey, and to bivouac at Sardar-Bulakh.
The order was given to march in half-col-
umn. It was perhaps the first time that an
English officer had ridden at the head of
these famous troops. We crossed the last
runnel on the southern edge of the plantation, and entered the silent waste.

For a while we slowly rode through the
camelthorn, the deep sand sinking beneath
our horses' feet. It was nearly one o'clock,
and the expanse around us streamed in the

full glare of noon. A spell seemed to rest
upon the landscape of the mountain, sealing all the springs of life. Only among
the evergreen shrubs about us a scattered
group of camels cropped the spinous foliage, little lizards darted, a flock of sand-
grouse took wing. Our course lay slantwise across the base of Ararat, toward the
hill of Takjaltu, a table-topped mass over-
grown with yellow herbage, which rises in
advance of the saddle between the mountains, and lies just below you as you overlook the landscape from the valley of
Sardar-Bulakh. Gullies of chalk, and
ground strewn with stones, succeed the
even surface of the belt of sand, and in
turn give way to the covering of burnt
grass which clothes the deep slope of the
great sweeping base, and encircles the fabric with a continuous stretch of ochre extending up the higher seams. Mile after
mile we rode at easy paces over the parched
turf and the cracking soil. When we had
accomplished a space of about ten miles,
and attained a height of nearly six thousand feet, the land broke about us into
miniature ravines, deep gullies strewn with
stones and bowlders, searing the slope about
the line of limit where the base may be
said to determine and the higher seams

begin. Winding down the sides of these
rocky hollows, one might turn in the saddle at a bend of the track, and observe the
long line of horsemen defiling into the
ravine. I noticed that by far the greater
number among them — if, indeed, one
might not say all — were men in the
opening years of manhood; lithe, well-
knit figures, and fair complexions set round
with fair hair. At a nearer view the feature which most impressed me was the
smallness of their eyes. They wear the
long-skirted coat of Circassia, a thin and
worn *kharki;* the faded pink on the cloth
of their shoulder-straps relieves the dull
drab. Their little caps of Circassian pattern fit closely round their heads. Their
horses are clumsy, long-backed creatures,
wanting in all the characteristics of quality; and as each man maintains his own
animal, few among them are shod. Yet
I am assured that the breed is workman-
like and enduring, and I have known it
to yield most satisfactory progeny when
crossed with English racing-blood. As
we rounded the heap of grass-grown soil,
which is known as Takjaltu, we were
joined by a second detachment of Cossacks coming from Arguri. Together we
climbed up the troughs of the ridges which

sweep fanwise down the mountain side, and emerged on the floor of the upland valley which leads between the Greater and the Lesser Ararat, and crosses the back of the Ararat fabric in a direction from southwest to northeast. We were here at an elevation of 7,500 feet above the sea, or nearly five thousand feet above the plain. Both the stony troughs and ridges up which we had just marched, as well as the comparatively level ground upon which we now stood, were covered with a scorched but abundant vegetation, which had served the Kurds during earlier summer as pasture for their flocks, and still sheltered numerous coveys of plump partridges, in which this part of the mountain abounds.

At the mouth of this valley, on the gently sloping platform which its even surface presents, we marked out the spaces of our bivouac, the pickets for the horses, and the fires. Our men were acquainted with every cranny; we had halted near the site of their summer encampment, from which they had only recently descended to their winter quarters in the plain. As we dismounted we were met by a graceful figure clad in a Circassian coat of brown material let in across the breast with pink silk,—a young man of most engaging ap-

Colossal Blocks of Conglomerate Hurled out of the Chasm of Arguri.

pearance and manners, presented to us as the chief of the Kurds of Ararat who own allegiance to the Tsar. In the high refinement of his features, in the bronzed complexion and soft brown eyes, the Kurd made a striking contrast to the Cossacks, — a contrast by no means to the advantage of the Cis-Caucasian race. The young chief is also worthy to be remembered in respect of the remarkable name which he bears. His Kurdish title of Shamden Agha has been developed and embroidered into the sonorous appellation of Hassan Bey Shamshadinoff, under which he is officially known.

From the edge of the platform upon which we were standing the ground falls away with some abruptness down to the base below, and lends to the valley its characteristic appearance of an elevated stage and natural viewing-place, overtowered by the summit regions of the dome and the pyramid, and commanding all the landscape of the plain. On the southwest, as it rises toward the pass between the two mountains,—a pass of 8,800 feet, leading into Turkish and into Persian territory, to Bayazed or Maku,—the extent of even ground which composes this platform cannot much exceed a quarter of a mile. It is choked by the rocky causeways which, sweeping down the side of Great Ararat, tumble headlong to the bottom of the fork, and, taking the inclination of the ever-widening valley, descend on the northwestern skirt of the platform in long oblique curves of branching troughs and ridges falling fanwise over the base. The width of the platform at the mouth of the valley may be about three-quarters of a mile. It is here that the Kurds of the surrounding region gather, as the shades of night approach, to water their flocks at the lonely pool which is known as the Sardar's well. On the summit of the Lesser Ar-

arat there is a little lake formed of melted
snows; the water permeates the mountain,
and feeds the Sardar's pool. Close by, at
the foot of the lesser mountain, is the
famous covert of birch, low bushes, the
only stretch of wood upon the fabric,
which is entirely devoid of trees. The
wood was soon crackling upon our fires,
and the water hissing in the pots; but the
wretched pack-horses upon which our tents
had been loaded were lagging several hours
behind. We ourselves had reached camp
at six o'clock ; it was after nine before our
baggage arrived. As we stretched upon the
slope, the keen air of the summit region
swept the valley, and chilled us to the skin;
the temperature sank to below freezing,
and we had nothing but the things in
which we stood.* Our friends, the Cossack officers, were lavish of assistance ;
they wrapped us in the hairy coats of the
Caucasus, placed *vodki* and partridges before us, and ranged us around their hospit-
able circle beside the leaping flames.

But the mind was absent from the picturesque bivouac, and the eye which ranged
the deepening shadows was still dazzled by
the evening lights. Mind and sense alike

* The temperature at 6.30 P.M. was 50° F., but it sank rapidly
in the cold wind.

were saturated with the beauty and the brilliance of the landscape, which, as you rise toward the edge of the platform after rounding the mass of Takjaltu, opens to an ever-increasing perspective with ever-growing clearness of essential features and mystery gathering upon all lesser forms. The sun revolving south of the zenith lights the mountains on the north of the plain, and fills all the valley from the slopes of Ararat with the full flood of its rays, — tier after tier of crinkled hummock ranges aligning the opposite margin of the valley at a distance of over twenty miles; their summits fretted with shapes of cones and craters, their faces buttressed in sand, bare and devoid of all vegetation, — yet richly clothed in lights and hues of fairyland, ochres flushed with delicate madder, amethyst shaded opaline, while the sparse plantations about the river and the labyrinth of the plain insensibly transfigure as you rise above them into an impalpable web of gray. In the lap of the landscape lies the river, a thin, looping thread, — flashes of white among the shadows, in the lights a bright mineral green. Here and there on its banks you descry a naked mound, — conjuring a vision of forgotten civilizations and the buried hives of man. It is a vast prospect over the world; yet vaster far is the expanse you feel about you, beyond the limits of sight. It is nothing but a segment of that expanse, a brief vista from north to east between two mountain-sides. On the north the slopes of Great Ararat hide the presence of Alagöz, while behind the needle form of Little Ararat all the barren chains and lonely valleys of Persia are outspread. The evening grows, and the sun's returning arc bends behind the dome of snow. The light falls between the two mountains, and connects the Little Ararat in a common harmony with the richening tints of the plain. There it stands on the farther margin of the platform, the clean, sharp outline of a pyramid, clothed in hues of a tender yellow seamed with violet veins. At its feet, where its train sweeps the floor of the river valley in long and regular folds, — far away in the east, toward the mists of the Caspian, — the sandy ground breaks into a troubled surface like angry waves set solid under a spell, and from range to range stretch a chain of low white hummocks like islands across a sea. Just there in the distance, beneath the Little Ararat, you see a patch of shining white, so vivid that it presents the appearance of a glacier set in the burnt waste. It is probably caused by some chemical efflorescence resting on the dry bed of a lake. All the landscape reveals the frenzy of volcanic forces fixed forever in an imperishable mould; the imagination plays with the forms of distant castles and fortresses of sand. Alone the slopes about you wear the solid colors, and hold you to the real world, — the massive slopes of Great Ararat raised high above the world. The wreath of cloud which veils the summit till the last breath of warm air dies, has floated away in the calm heaven before the western lights have paled. Behind the lofty piles of rocky causeways, concealing the higher seams, rises the immediate roof of Ararat, foreshortened in the sky, the short side or gable of the dome, a faultless cone of snow.

When we drew aside the curtain of our tent next morning, full daylight was streaming over the open upland valley, and the vigorous air had already lost its edge.* The sun had risen high above the Sevanga ranges, and swept the plain below us of the lingering vapors which at morning cling, like shining wool, to the floor of the river-valley, or float in rosy feathers against the dawn. The long-backed Cos-

* Temperature. 10.15 A.M., 72° F.

sack horses had been groomed and watered
and picketed in line ; the men were sitting
smoking in little groups, or were strolling
about the camp in pairs.   A few Kurds,
who had come down with milk and provisions, stood listlessly looking on, the beak-
nose projecting from the bony cheeks, the
brown chest opening from the many-colored tatters draped about the shoulders and
waist.   The space of level ground between
the two mountains cannot much exceed
three-quarters of a mile.   On the east the
graceful seams of Little Ararat rise immediately from the slope upon our right,
gathering just beyond the cover of low
birchwood, and converging in the form
of a pyramid toward a summit which has
been broken across the point.   The platform of this valley is a base for Little
Ararat, the rib on the flank of the greater
mountain from which the smaller proceeds.
So sharp are the lines of the Little Ararat,
so clean the upward slope, that the summit,
when seen from this pass or saddle, seems
to rise as high in the heaven above as the
dome of Great Ararat itself.   The burnt
grass struggles toward the little birch cover, but scarcely touches the higher seams.
The mountain-side is broken into a loose
rubble ; deep gullies sear it in perpendic-

ular furrows, which contribute to the impression of height. The prevailing color of the stones is a bleached yellow, verging upon a delicate pink ; but these paler strata are divided by veins of bluish andesite, pointing upward like spear-heads from the base.

Very different on the side of Great Ararat are the shapes which meet the eye. We are facing the southeastern slope of the mountain, the slope which follows the direction of its axis, the short side or gable of the dome. In the descending train of the giant volcano this valley is but an incidental or lesser feature ; yet it marks, and in a sense determines, an important alteration in the disposition of the surface forms. It is here that the streams of molten matter descending the mountain-side have been arrested, and deflected from their original direction to fall over the massive base. The dam or obstacle which has produced this deviation is the sharp harmonious figure of the Lesser Ararat, emerging from the sea of piled-up bowlders, and cleaving the chaos of troughs and ridges like the lofty prow of a ship. The course of these streams of lava is signalized by these causeways of agglomerate rocks ; you may follow from a point of vantage upon the mountain the numerous branches into which they have divided, to several parent or larger streams. On this side of Ararat they have been turned in an oblique direction, from the southeast toward the northeast; and they skirt the western margin of the little valley, curving outward to the river and the plain. It is just beneath the first of these walls of loose bowlders that our two little tents are pitched; beyond it you see another and yet another still higher, and above them the dome of snow.

The distance from this valley to the summit of Great Ararat, if we measure upon the survey of the Russian Government along a horizontal line, is rather over five miles. The confused sea of bowlders, of which I have just described the nature, extends, according to my own measurements, to a height of about twelve thousand feet. Above that zone, so arduous to traverse, lies the summit region of the mountain, robed in perpetual snow. From whatever point you regard that summit on this southeastern side, the appearance of its height falls short of reality in a most substantial degree. Not only does the curve of the upward slope lend itself to a most deceitful foreshortening when you follow it from below, but indeed the highest point or crown of the dome is invisible from this the gable side.

If you strike a direct course from the encampment toward the roof of snow, and crossing the grain of successive walls and depressions, emerge upon some higher ridge, the numerous ramifications of the lava system may be followed to their source, and are seen to issue from larger causeways, which rise in bold relief from the snows of the summit region, and open fanwise down the higher slopes. In shape these causeways may be said to resemble the sharp side of a wedge: the massive base from which the bank rises narrows to a pointed spine. As the eye pursues the circle of the summit where it vanishes toward the north, these ribs of rock which radiate down the mountain diminish in volume and relief. Their sharp edges commence to cut the snowy canopy about three thousand feet below the dome. It is rather on the southeastern side of Ararat, the side which faces the Little Ararat and follows the direction of the axis of the fabric,—the line upon which the forces have acted by which the whole fabric has been reared,—that a formation so characteristic of the surface of the summit region attains its highest development in a phenomenon

Lesser Ararat as it appeared just before reaching Sardar-Bulakh.

which at once arrests the eye. At a height
of about fourteen thousand feet a causeway
of truly gigantic proportions breaks abruptly from the snow. The head of the ridge
is bold and lofty, and towers high above
the snow-slope, with steep and rocky sides.
The ridge itself is in form a wedge or triangle cut deep down into the side of the
mountain, and marked along the spine by
a canal-shaped depression which accentu-
ates the descending curve. The zone of
troughs and ridges which you are now
crossing has its origin in this parent ridge;

you see it sweeping outward, away from Little Ararat, and dividing into branches, and systems of branches, as it reaches the lower slopes. Whether its want of connection with the roof of Ararat, or the inherent characteristics of its uppermost end, are sufficient evidence to justify the supposition of Abich, that this ridge at its head marks a separate eruptive centre on the flank of Ararat, I am not competent adequately to discuss. I can only observe, that another explanation does not appear difficult to find : it may be possible that the ridge where it narrows to the summit has been fractured and swept away. This peak, or sharp end of the causeway, to whatever causes its origin may be ascribed, is a distinguishing feature on the slope of Ararat, seen far and wide like a tooth or hump or shoulder on this the southeastern side. Although the most direct way to the summit region leads immediately across the zone of bowlders from the camp by the Sardar's pool, yet it is not that which most travellers have followed, or which the natives of the district recommend. This line of approach, which I followed for some distance a few days after our ascent, is open to the objection that it is no doubt more difficult to scale the slope of snow

upon this side. The tract of uncovered
rocks which breaks the snow-fields, offering ladders to the roof of the dome, is
situated farther to the southeast of the
mountain, above the neck of the valley
of the pool. Whether it would not be
more easy to reach these ladders by skirting slantwise from the higher slopes is a
question which is not in itself unreason-
able, and which only actual experience
will decide. It was in this manner, I
believe, that the English traveller, Bryce,
— now the well-known writer upon the
American Commonwealth, and a statesman
of great authority and weight, — made an
ascent which, as a feat, is, I think, the
most remarkable of any of the recorded
climbs. Starting from the pool at one
o'clock in the morning, he reached the
summit alone at about two in the afternoon, accomplishing, within a space of
about six hours, the last five thousand feet,
and returning to the point from which he
started before sunrise on the following day.
We ourselves were advised to follow up the
valley, keeping the causeways upon our
right; and only then, when we should have
reached a point about southeast of the summit, to strike across the belt of rock.

At twenty minutes before two on the

18th of September, our little party left camp in marching order, all in the pride of health and spirits, and eager for the attack. Thin wreaths of cloud wrapped the snows of the summit, the jealous spell which baffles the bold lover, even when he already grasps his prize. We had taken leave of the Cossack officers and their band of light-hearted men. Our friends were returning to Arguri and Aralykh; the one body to hunt the Kurds of the frontier, the other to languish in dull inactivity until their turn shall come round again. Four Cossacks were deputed to remain and guard our camp; we ourselves had decided to dispense with any escort, and to trust to our Kurdish allies. Of these, ten sturdy fellows accompanied us as porters, to carry our effects, their rifles slung over their many-colored tatters beside the burden allotted to each. With my cousin and myself were the young Swiss, Rudolph Taugwalder, a worthy example of his race and profession, — the large limbs, the rosy cheeks, the open mien without guile, — and young Ernest Wesson, fresh from the Polytechnic in London, whom I had brought to develop my photographs, and who rendered me valuable assistance in my photographic work. My Armenian dragoman followed as best he was able, until the camp at the snow was reached; his plump little figure was not well adapted to toil over the giant rocks. Of our number was also an Armenian from Arguri, who had tendered his services as guide; he was able to indicate a place for our night's encampment, but he did not venture upon the slope of snow.

A little stream trickles down the valley, but sinks exhausted at this season before reaching the Sardar's well. In the early summer it is of the volume of a torrent, which winds past the encampment like a serpent of silver, uttering a dull, rumbling sound.* It is fed by the water from the snow-fields, and there is said to be a spring which contributes to support it at a height of nearly eleven thousand feet.† After half an hour's walk over the stony surface of the platform and the ragged herbage burnt yellow by the sun, we entered the narrows of the mountain saddle, and followed the dry bed of this rivulet at the foot of rocky spurs. The tufts of sappy grass, which were sparsely studded on the margin of the watercourse, gave

* Madame B. Chantre, in "Tour du Monde" for 1892, p. 184.
† Markoff: "Ascension du Grand Ararat," in *Bulletin de la Soc. Royale Belge de Géographie*, Brussels, 1888, p. 579.

place, as we advanced, to a continuous carpet of soft and verdant turf; here and there the eye rested on the deep green of the juniper, or the graceful fretwork of a wild-rose tree quivered in the draught. The warm rays flashed in the thin atmosphere, and tempered the searching breeze. The spurs on our right descend from the shoulder, and from the causeway of which it forms the head, and are seen to diverge into two systems as they enter the narrow pass. The one group pushes forward to the Little Ararat, and is lost in confused detail; the other, and perhaps the larger, system bends boldly along the side of the valley, sweeping outwards toward the base. At three o'clock we reached a large pool of clouded water collected on a table surface of burnt grass; close by is an extensive bed of nettles and a circle of loose stones. This spot is no doubt the site of a Kurdish encampment, and appeared to have been only recently abandoned by the shepherds and their flocks. The farther we progressed, the more the prospect opened over the slopes of Ararat; we were approaching the level of the lofty ridges which skirt the valley side. Passing, as we now were, between the two Ararats, we remarked that the greater seemed no higher than

Mount Ararat as seen from the Village of Aralykh (the Town in the foreground).
Taken at a height of 1,756 feet above sea-level and about seventeen miles from the mountain.

the lesser, so completely is the eye deceived. In the hollows of the gully, there were little pools of water, but the stream itself was dry.

By half-past three we had left the gentle watercourse, and were winding inwards up the slope of Great Ararat, to cross the black and barren region, the girdle of sharp crags and slippery bowlders drawn deep about the upper seams of the mountain like a succession of *chevaux-de-frise*. We thought it must have been on some other side of Ararat that the animals descended from the Ark. For a space of more than three hours we labored on over a chaos of rocks, through a labyrinth of ridges and troughs, picking a path, and as often retracing it, or scrambling up the polished sides of the larger blocks which arrest the most crafty approach. The Kurds, although sorely taxed by their burdens, were at an advantage compared to ourselves; they could slip like cats from ledge to ledge in their laced slippers of hide. In one place we passed a gigantic heap of bowlders towering several hundred feet above our heads. The rock is throughout of the same character and color, — an andesitic lava of a dark slaty hue. A little later we threaded up a ravine or gully, and after keeping for a while to the bottom of the depression, climbed slowly along the back of the ridge. I noticed that the grain or direction of the formation lay toward east-southeast. From the head of this ravine we turned into a second, by a natural gap or pass; loose rocks were piled along the sides of the hollow, which bristled with fantastic shapes. Here a seated group of camels seemed to munch in silence on the line of fading sky, or the knotty forms of lifeless willows stretched a menace of uplifted arms. In the sheltered laps of this higher region, as we approached our journey's end, the snow still lay in ragged patches, increasing in volume and depth. . . . The surface cleared, the view opened; we emerged from the troubled sea of stone. Beyond a lake of snow and a stretch of rubble, rose the ghostly sheet of the summit region holding the last glimmer of day.

It was seven o'clock, and we had no sooner halted than the biting frost numbed our limbs.* The ground about us was not uneven, but an endless crop of pebbles filled the plainer spaces between little capes of embedded rock. At length, upon the margin of the snow-lake, we found a tiny

* Temperature at 8 P.M. 18° F., and next morning at 5.45 A.M., 28° F.

tongue of turf-grown soil, just sufficient emplacement to hold the flying tent which we had brought for the purpose of this lofty bivouac near the line of continuous snow. We were five to share the modest area which the sloping canvas enclosed, yet the temperature in the tent sank below freezing before the night was done. Down the slope beside us, the snow-water trickled beneath a thin covering of ice. The sheepskin coats which we had brought from Aralykh protected us from chill, but the hardy Kurds slept in their seamy tatters upon the naked rocks around. One among them sought protection as the cold became intenser, and we wrapped him in a warm cape. It was the first time I had passed the night at so great an elevation, — 12,194 feet above the sea; and it is possible that the unwonted rarity of the atmosphere contributed to keep us awake. But whether it arose from the conditions which surrounded us, or from a nervous state of physical excitement inspired by our enterprise, not one among us, excepting the dragoman, succeeded in courting sleep. That plump little person had struggled on bravely to this, his farthest goal; and his heavy breathing fell upon the silence of the calm, transparent night.

Panorama of Mount Ararat.

The site of our camp below the snow-line marks a new stage or structural division in the fabric of Ararat. Of these divisions, which differ from one another not only in the characteristics presented by each among them, but also in the gradient of slope, it is natural to distinguish three. We are dealing in particular with that section of the mountain which lies between Aralykh and the summit, and with the features of the southeastern side. First there is the massive base of the mountain, about ten miles in depth, extending from the floor of the river-valley to a

as Viewed from Aralykh.

height of about six thousand feet. At
that point the higher seams commence to
gather, and the belt of rock begins. The
arduous tracts which we had just traversed,
where large, loose blocks of hard black
lava are piled up like a beach, compose
the upper portion of this middle region,
and may be said to touch the lower margin of the continuous fields of snow. But
the line of contact between the extremi-
ties of the one and the other stage is by
no means so clear and so definite a feature
as our metaphor might lead us to expect,
and partakes of the nature of a transitional

system, a neutral zone on the mountain-
side, where the rocky layers of the middle
slopes have not yet shelved away, nor the
immediate seams of the summit region
settled to their long climb.   In this sense
the stone-fields about our encampment,
with their patches of last year's snow, are
invested with the attributes of a natural
threshold at the foot of the great dome.
The stage which is highest in the structure of Ararat, the stage which holds the
dome, has its origin in this threshold or
neutral district at an altitude which varies
between twelve thousand and thirteen
thousand feet.

Very different in character and in appearance from the region we are leaving
behind is the slope which faces our encampment robed in perpetual snow.   We
have pursued the ramifications of the lava
system to the side of their parent stems;
and in place of blind troughs and prospect-
less ledges, a noble singleness of feature
breaks upon the extricated view.   We
command the whole summit structure of
Ararat on the short or gable side, and the
shape which rises from the open ground
about us is that of a massive cone.   The
regular seams which mount to the summit
stretch continuous to the crown of snow,

and are inclined at an angle which diverges very little from an average of 30°. The gradients from which these higher seams gather, the slopes about our camp, cannot exceed half that inclination, or an angle of 15°. Such is the outline, so harmonious and simple, which a first glance reveals. A more intimate study of the summit region as it expands to a closer view, discloses characteristics which are not exactly similar to those with which we have already become familiar in the neighborhood of Sardar-Bulakh. It was there the northeastern hemisphere of the mountain — if the term may be applied to the oval figure which the summit region presents — displayed to the prospect upon the segment between east and southeast. Our present position lies more to the southward, between the two hemispheres; we are placed near the axis of the figure, and the roof, as seen from our encampment, bears nearly due northwest. The gigantic causeway which was there descending on our left hand from the distant snows, now rises on our right like a rocky headland confronting a gleaming sea of ice. But when the eye pursues the summit circle vanishing towards the west, we miss the sister forms of lesser causeways radiating down the mountain-side. It is true that the greater proximity of our standpoint to the foot of these highest slopes curtails the segment of the circle which we are able to command. This circumstance is not in itself sufficient to explain the change in the physiognomy of the summit region as we see it on this side. In place of those bold black ribs or ridges spread fanwise down the incline, furrowing the snows with their sharp edges, and lined along the troughs of their contiguous bases with broad streaks of sheltered *névé*, it seems as if the fabric had fallen asunder, the surface slipped away, all the flank of the mountain depressed and hollow from our camp to the roof of the dome. The canopy of snow which encircles the summit, a broad inviolate bank unbroken by any rift or rock projection for a depth of some two thousand feet, breaks sharply off on the verge of this depression, and leaves the shallow cavity bare. From the base of the giant causeway just above us to the gently pursing outline of the roof, you follow the edge of the great snow-field bordering a rough and crumbling region which offers scanty foothold to the snow, where the hollow slope bristles with pointed bowlders, and the bold crags pierce the ruin around them in upstanding combs or saw-shaped ridges holding slantwise to the mountain-side. On the west side of this broad and uncovered depression, near the western extremity of the cone, a long strip of snow descends from the summit, caught by some trough or sheltering fissure in the rough face of the cliff. Beyond it, just upon the skyline, the bare rocks reappear, and climb the slope like a natural ladder to a point where the roof of the dome is lowest, and appears to offer the readiest access to the still invisible crown.

In the attenuated atmosphere surrounding the summit, every foot that is gained tells; an approach which promises to ease the gradient at the time when it presses most seems to offer advantages which some future traveller, recognizing the application of this description, may be encouraged to essay. We ourselves were influenced in the choice of a principle upon which to base our attack by the confident counsels of the Armenian, which the local knowledge of the Kurds confirmed. We were advised to keep to the eastern margin of the depression by the edge of the great snow-field. You see the brown rocks still baffling the snowdrifts near the point where the deceitful slope appears to end, where on the verge of the roof it just dips a little, then stands up like a low white wall on the luminous ground of blue.

The troubled sea of bowlders flowing toward the Little Ararat, from which we had just emerged, still hemmed us in from any prospect over the tracts which lay below. The flush of dawn broke between the two mountains from a narrow vista of sky. The even surface of the snow slope loomed white and cold above our heads, while the night still lingered on the dark stone about us, shadowing the little laps of ice. Before six o'clock we were afoot and ready; it wanted a few minutes to the hour as we set out from our camp. To the Swiss was intrusted the post of leader; behind him followed, in varying order, my cousin and Wesson and myself. Slowly we passed from the shore of the snow lake to the gathering of the higher seams, harboring our strength for the steeper gradients, as we made across the beach of bowlders, stepping firmly from block to block. The broad white sheet of the summit circle descends to the snow-lakes of the lower region in a tongue or gulf of deep *névé*. You may follow, on the margin of the great depression, the western edge of this gleaming surface unbroken down the side of the cone. On the east the

black wall of the giant causeway aligns
the shining slope, invading the field of perpetual winter to a height of over 14,000
feet. The width of the snow-field between
these limits varies as it descends. On a level
with the shoulder or head of the causeway
it appeared to span an interval of nearly
two hundred yards. The depth of the bed
must be considerable; and, while the surface holds the tread in places, it as often
gives, and lets you through. No rock projection or gap or fissure breaks the slope
of the white fairway; but the winds have
raised the crust about the centre into a ribbon of tiny waves. Our plan was to cross
the stony region about us, slanting a little
east, and then when we should have reached
the edge of the snow-field, to mount by the
rocks on its immediate margin, adhering
as closely as might be possible to the side
of the snow. It was in the execution of
this plan, so simple in its conception, that
the trained instinct of the Swiss availed.
Of those who have attempted the ascent of
Ararat,—and their number is not large,—
so many have failed to reach the summit,
that, upon a mountain which makes few,
if any, demands upon the resources of the
climber's craft, their discomfiture must be
attributed to other reasons,—to the pecu-

liar nature of the ground traversed no less
than to the inordinate duration of the effort,
to the wearisome recurrence of the same
kind of obstacles, and to the rarity of the air.
Now the disposition of the rocks upon the
surface of the depression is by no means the
same as that which we have studied in connection with the seams which lie below.
The path no longer struggles across a troubled sea of ridges, or strays within the blind
recesses of a succession of gigantic waves
of stone. On the other hand, the gradients
are, as a rule, steeper ; and the clearings are
covered with a loose rubble, which slips
from under the feet. The bowlders are
piled one upon another in heaps, as they
happened to fall; and the sequence of forms
is throughout arbitrary, and subject to no
fixed law. In one place it is a tower of
this loose masonry which blocks all farther
approach, in another a solid barrier of sharp
crags laced together which it is necessary
to circumvent. When the limbs have been
stiffened and the patience exhausted by the
long and devious escalade, the tax upon
the lungs is at its highest, and the strain
upon the heart most severe. Many of the
difficulties which travellers have encountered upon this stage of the climb may be
avoided, or met at a greater advantage, by

The Ascent of Mount Ararat

Kurd Porters.

adhering to the edge of the snow. But
the fulfilment of this purpose is by no means
so easy as the case might at first sight appear. You are always winding inwards to
avoid the heaps of bowlders, or emerging
on the backs of gigantic blocks of lava towards the margin of the shining slope. In
the choice of the most direct path, where
many offered, the Swiss was never at fault;
he made up the cone without a moment's
hesitation, like a hound threading a close
cover, and seldom if ever foiled.

At twenty minutes to seven, when the
summit of Lesser Ararat was about on a
level with the eye, we paused for awhile,
and turned towards the prospect now opening to a wider range. The day was clear,
and promised warmth; above us the snowy
dome of Ararat shone in a cloudless sky.
The landscape on either side of the beautiful pyramid lay outspread at our feet;
from northeast the hidden shores of Lake
Sevanga, to where the invisible seas of Van
and Urumia diffuse a soft veil of opaline
vapor over the long succession of lonely
ranges in the southeast and south. The
wild borderland of Persia and Turkey
here for the first time expands to view.
The scene, however much it may belie
the conception at a first and hasty glance,

bears the familiar imprint of the characteristics peculiar to the great table-land. The mountains reveal their essential nature, and disclose the familiar forms, the surface of the plateau broken into long furrows which tend to hummock shapes. So lofty is the stage, so aloof this mighty fabric from all surrounding forms, the world lies dim and featureless about it like the setting of a dream. In the foreground are the valleys on the south of Little Ararat circling round to the Araxes floor, and on the northeast, beside the thread of the looping river, a little lake, dropped like a turquoise on the sand where the mountain sweeps the plain.

In the space of another hour we have reached an elevation about equal to that of the head of the causeway on the opposite side of the snow, a point which I think I am justified in fixing at over fourteen thousand feet. We are now no longer threading on the shore of an inlet; alone the vague horizon of the summit circle is the limit of the broad white sea. But on our left hand the snowless region of rock and rubble still accompanies our course, and a group of red crags stands high above us where the upward slope appears to end.

Yet another two hours of continuous

climbing, and at about half-past nine the loose bowlders about us open, and we are approaching the foot of these crags. The end seems near; but the slope is deceitful, and when once we have reached the head of the formation the long white way resumes. But the blue vault about us streams with sunlight; the snow is melting in the crannies, a genial spirit lightens our toil.

And now without any sign or warning the mysterious spell which holds the mountain begins to throw a web about us, craftily, from below. The spirits of the air come sailing through the azure with shining gossamer wings, while the heavier vapors gather around us from dense banks serried upon the slope beneath us a thousand feet lower down.

The rocks still climb the increasing gradient, but the snow is closing in. At eleven we halt to copy an inscription which has been neatly written in Russian characters on the face of a bowlder-stone. It records that on the third day of the eighth month of 1893 the expedition led by the Russian traveller Postukhoff passed the night in this place. At the foot of the stone lie several objects; a bottle filled with fluid, an empty biscuit-tin, and a tin containing specimens of rock.

At half-past eleven I take the angle of the snow-slope, at this point 35°. About this time the Swiss thinks it prudent to link us all together with his rope. The surface of the rocks is still uncovered, but their bases are embedded in deep snow.

It is now, after six hours arduous climbing, that the strain of the effort tells. The lungs are working at the extreme of their capacity, and the pressure upon the heart is severe. At noon I call a halt, and release young Wesson from his place in the file of four. His pluck is still strong, but his look and gait alarm me, and I persuade him to desist. We leave him to rest in a sheltered place, and there await our return. From this time on we all three suffer, even the Swiss himself. My cousin is affected with mountain sickness; as for me, I find it almost impossible to breathe and climb at the same time. We make a few steps upwards, and then pause breathless, and gasp again and again. The white slope vanishing above us must end in the crown of the dome; and the bowlders, strewn more sparsely before us, promise a fairer way. But the farther we go the goal seems little closer, and the shallow snow resting on a crumbling rubble makes us lose one step in every three. A strong smell of sulphur permeates the atmosphere; it proceeds from the sliding surface upon which we are treading, a detritus of pale sulphurous stones.

At 1.25 P.M. we see a plate of white metal affixed to a cranny in the rocks. It bears an inscription in Russian character, which dates from 1888. I neglect to copy out the unfamiliar letters; but there can be little doubt that they record the successful ascent of Dr. Markoff, an ascent in which that able linguist and accomplished traveller suffered hardships which cost him dear.

A few minutes later, at half-past one, the slope at last eases, the ground flattens, the struggling rocks sink beneath the surface of a continuous field of snow. At last we stand upon the summit of Ararat; but the sun no longer pierces the white vapor. A fierce gale drives across the forbidden region, and whips the eye straining to distinguish the limits of snow and cloud. Vague forms hurry past on the wings of the whirlwind; in place of the landscape of the land of promise, we search dense banks of fog.

Disappointed, perhaps, but relieved of the gradient, and elated with the success of our climb, we run in the teeth of the wind across the platform, our feet scarcely sinking in the storm-swept crust of the surface, the gently undulating roof of the dome. . . . Along the edge of a spacious snow-field which dips towards the centre, and is longest from northwest to southeast, on the vaulted rim of the saucer, which the surface resembles, four separate elevations may conveniently be distinguished as the highest points in the irregular oval figure which the whole platform appears to present. The highest among these rounded elevations bears northwest from the spot where we first touch the summit or emerge upon the roof. That spot itself marks another of these inequalities; the remaining two are situated respectively in this manner,—the one about midway between the two already mentioned, but nearer to the first, and on the north side; the other about south of the northwestern elevation, and this seems the lowest of all. The difference in height between this northwestern elevation and that upon the southeast is about two hundred feet; and the length of the figure between these points—we paced only a certain portion of the distance—is about five hundred yards. The width of the platform, so far as we could gauge it, may be some three hundred yards. A sin-

gle object testifies to the efforts of our fore-
runners, and to the insatiable enterprise of
man, — a stout stake embedded upon the
northwestern elevation in a little pyramid
of stones. It is here that we take our
observations and make our longest halt.*
Before us lies a valley or deep depression,
and on the farther side rises the northwestern summit, a symmetrical cone of
snow. This summit connects with the
bold snow buttresses beyond it, terraced
upon the northwestern slope. The distance down and up from where we stand
to that summit may be about four hundred yards; but neither the Swiss nor
ourselves consider it higher, and we are
prevented from still further exploring the
summit region by the increasing violence
of the gale and by the gathering gloom of
cloud. The sides and floor of the valley or
saddle between the two summits are completely covered with snow; and we see no
trace of the lateral fissure which Abich —
no doubt under different circumstances —
was able to observe.

* The temperature of the air a few feet below the summit,
out of the gale, was 20° F. The height of the northwestern elevation of the southeastern summit of Ararat is given by my
Whymper mountain aneroid as 17,493 feet. The reading is, no
doubt, too high by several hundred feet. The Carey aneroid
gives a still higher figure, and the Boylean-Mariotte mercurial
barometer entirely refused to work.

We remain forty minutes upon the summit; but the dense veil never lifts from the platform, nor does the blast cease to pierce us through. No sooner does an opening in the driving vapors reveal a vista of the world below than fresh levies fly to the unguarded interval, and the wild onset resumes. Yet what if the spell had lost its power, and the mountain and the world lain bare? had the tissue of the air beamed clear as crystal, and the forms of earth and sea, embroidered beneath us, shone like the tracery of a shield?

We should have gained a balloon view over nature; should we catch her voice so well? the ancient voice heard at cool of day in the garden, or the voice that spoke in accents of thunder to a world condemned to die. " It repented the Lord that he had made man, and it grieved him at his heart. The earth was filled with violence. God looked upon the earth, and behold it was corrupt. In the second month, the seventeenth day of the month, the same day were all the fountains of the great deep broken up, and the windows of heaven were opened. And the rain was upon the earth forty days and forty nights."

We are standing on the spot where the

Ark of Gopher rested, where first the patri-
arch alighted on the face of an earth renewed. Before him lie the valleys of six
hundred years of sorrow; the airiest pinnacle supports him, a boundless hope fills
his eyes; the pulse of life beats strong
and fresh around him; the busy swarms
thrill with sweet freedom, elect of all living things. In the settling exhalations
stands the bow of many colors, eternal
token of God's covenant with man.

The peaks which rise on the distant
borderland where silence has first faltered
into speech are wrapped about with the
wreaths of fancy, — a palpable world of
cloud. Do we fix our foot upon these
solid landmarks to wish the vague away,
to see the hard summits stark and naked,
and all the floating realm of mystery flown?
The truth is firm, and it is well to touch
and feel it, and know where the legend
begins; but the legend itself is truth trans-
figured as the snow distils into cloud. The
reality of life speaks in every syllable of
that solemn, stately tale, — divine hope
bursting the bounds of matter to com-
promise with despair. And the ancient
mountain summons the spirits about him,
and veils a futile frown as the rising sun
illumines the valleys of Asia and the life of

man lies bare. The spectres walk in naked daylight, — Violence and Corruption and Decay. The traveller finds in majestic nature consolation for these sordid scenes, while a spirit seems to whisper in his ears, "Turn from him! turn from him, that he may rest till he shall accomplish, as an hireling, his day."

CLIMBING MOUNT ST. ELIAS

By William Williams

Landing through the Surf at Icy Bay.

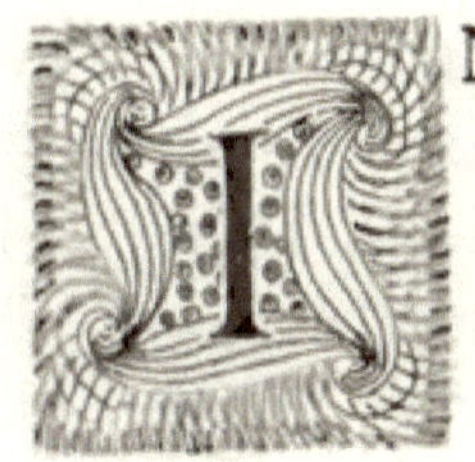N 1886 the *New York Times* organized an expedition under Lieutenant Schwatka, the main object of which was to explore the glaciers to the southward of Mount St. Elias, and ascend the mountain as far as possible. This was the first attempt ever made to penetrate that part of Alaska. The party succeeded in getting within two or three miles of the foot of the mountain, which lies at a distance of about thirty-five miles from the sea; but owing to the un-

favorable state of the weather, combined with other causes, all attempts to ascend Mount St. Elias proper were abandoned. Mr. Seton-Karr, however, climbed one of a chain of hills situated in the vicinity of the main range. Only nine or ten days were spent away from the beach.

In the spring of 1888, Mr. Harold W. Topham, of London, came over to this country with his brother, with a view to getting up an expedition similar in its purpose to that sent out by the *Times*. I was fortunate in receiving an invitation to join them. Later, a third Englishman, Mr. George Broke, was added to the party; and by the end of June we were all at Sitka, ready to avail ourselves of the first opportunity to proceed north.

The Schwatka party were spared much time and trouble in getting up the coast, as the U. S. S. Pinta had received orders to carry them as far as they wished to go. Not being so fortunate in this respect, we were obliged to proceed partly by sailing vessel, partly by canoes. The only available vessel was the Alpha, a very indifferent schooner of twenty-seven tons, which had just returned from a sealing cruise. After some delay in getting her ready, we set sail from Sitka on the 3d of July, the

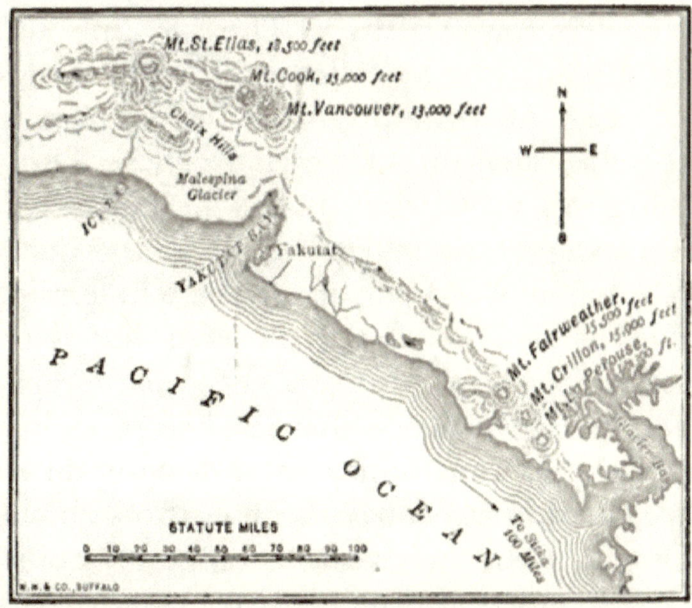

The Alaskan Coast from Mount Fairweather to Mount St. Elias.

party then consisting of ourselves and six
packers, two of whom were white men,
and the remaining four Indians. Though
the latter are generally capable of carrying
heavier loads than white men, yet we did
not think it advisable to rely on them altogether, lest they should leave us suddenly
in the lurch.

We were seven days in reaching Yakutat,
an Indian settlement situated two hundred
and fifty miles beyond Sitka. (See map
above.) The voyage was anything but enjoyable. The winds were generally light,
and from an unfavorable quarter, while

the vessel was filthy. The cooking was all done in the so-called cabin; and in order that no time might be lost in starting the fire, coal-oil was used freely. There being no ventilation, it can be said without exaggeration that the air in the quarters below was foul during the whole trip; which, as we suffered more or less from seasickness, constituted a very poor preparation for the work that lay before us.

On the fourth day after leaving Sitka we caught occasional glimpses through the clouds of the Fairweather range of mountains, consisting principally of Mount Fairweather, Mount Crillon, and Mount La Pérouse. These peaks rise almost directly out of the sea, two of them to a height of nearly sixteen thousand feet. I obtained a fine view of them on the return trip, and have no hesitation in saying that they present one of the grandest of mountain panoramas. Owing partly to their proximity, they appear much finer than from Glacier Bay, from which point many Alaskan tourists see them yearly. Several glaciers descend from their slopes, some of which, as that at Icy Point, terminate abruptly in the ocean, their faces, which are washed by the sea, being about two miles long. On Mount Crillon we noticed in particular

two icefalls that impressed us as being unusually fine.

Yakutat Bay is the first indentation of
any importance above Cross Sound, and
hence is easily recognized in clear weather.
The coast to the eastward is very low, and
generally lined with pine-trees. Yakutat
itself is situated on a small island about
five miles up the bay. It has a fairly good
harbor, the entrance to which is by means
of a channel not over twenty yards wide.
It is exclusively an Indian settlement, and
consists of just five houses, each covering
an area of perhaps thirty square feet. They
are quite picturesque, a distinctive feature
being the oval door, which is none too
large, and situated a foot or more above
the outside platform, so that in order to
enter, one must reduce one's height at both
ends. The houses are all of a size, and
contain a large central space which serves
both as parlor and kitchen. Opening out
on it are several smaller rooms, which are
allotted to the different families. The
chief, Billy, is quite friendly, and will
allow one, if without shelter, to spend
several days in his house. If he expects
anything in return, he will say so beforehand.

The inhabitants evinced a sort of stupid

interest at our coming. One, "Dick the Dude," of Juneau, whom we had temporarily hired at Sitka, but soon afterward discharged, as being too true to his nickname, had, in order to annoy us, sent up word of our arrival by some Indians who were coming north in canoes to visit their friends, stating that we were very anxious to obtain packers, and were ready to pay high wages. As a result, the Yakutats stood out for three dollars a day for some time. Fortunately we were not altogether dependent on them; and the realization of this fact, more than anything else, brought them to terms. We eventually hired two of them at two dollars a day, and further increased our party by the addition of two more white men, who were to receive three dollars a day. We then numbered fourteen.

The next stage in our journey was from Yakutat to Icy Bay, situated about fifty-five miles to the northwest. No one, however, should be misled by the word "Bay;" for, as we subsequently learned, the curvature of the beach is almost imperceptible, and hence offers no protection against the ocean swell which is constantly sweeping in. We were obliged to proceed thither in canoes, on account of the surf through which we had to land. The canoes used along the Alaskan coast are "dug-outs;" they are made of all sizes. As but few trees are of sufficient thickness to give the large ones the requisite beam, the sides are stretched, and made to retain their new position by means of water heated by stones.

The Indians acted in a very aggravating manner about starting. Not caring to paddle their canoes fifty-five miles, it was their intention to wait for a fair off-shore breeze. Our main object, on the other hand, was to reach Icy Bay while the surf was low, re-

Cutting Steps up an Ice Slope.

gardless of whether a fair wind was blowing or not. Why we should be in any hurry was quite incomprehensible to men to whom time is no object. We finally succeeded in making them do as we pleased by threatening to proceed in the Alpha.

We left Yakutat on the morning of July 13 in two large canoes and one small one, all three being very heavily laden with men and provisions. The trip to Icy Bay was accomplished in ten hours, thanks to an off-shore breeze which sprang up early in the morning and stayed by us most of the day. Part of the time, and for a distance of over fifteen miles, we were sailing along the foot of the Malespina Glacier, so covered with earth, stones, and brush as to make it absolutely impossible to discern the ice with the eye, though the temperature of both wind and water gave clear evidence of its presence.

Sailing in a large canoe is a most delightful experience. The craft seems to glide over the surface of the water without cutting it. This is owing to its very light draught. Its great width, on the other hand, gives it considerable stability up to a certain point. If the Indians were taught the use of the folding centre-board, they could probably make their canoes go fairly well to windward. The best they can do now is to avail themselves of a beam-wind.

We found comparatively little surf anywhere on the coast, and by awaiting their opportunity the Indians succeeded, amidst the most intense excitement on their part, in bringing the canoes in on the crest of a wave, and landing us without much wetting. Fifteen hours after our arrival the surf, however, was so high that it would have been impossible for us to reach the beach in safety. We landed very near the place where the Schwatka party were put ashore by the Pinta's boats. The beach at this point is broad and steep, and composed of dark sand, which, together with the dark green trees in the background, gave the landscape a sombre and impressive appearance.

It may now be well to say a word about our general plans. We had brought along fourteen hundred pounds of provisions, consisting mainly of bacon, hams, smoked salmon, flour, beans, dried apples, tea, and coffee, enough to enable fourteen men to remain away from Yakutat forty days if necessary. Of these forty days it was our intention to devote at the outside twenty-eight to climbing. Food had been brought for the remaining twelve, in case we should be detained at Icy Bay on our return through the unfavorable condition of the surf, as we could not count on obtaining

Mount St. Elias from the Northwest Corner of the Chaix Hills.

any food at that place except seal meat or
blubber, which we tried, and found wanting.   Hence it was never intended to remove more than about two-thirds of our
provisions from the beach.

On the morning of the 16th we broke
camp, leaving an Indian behind to take
care of the canoes which remained.   We
regretted having to place ourselves to such
an extent in the power of an Indian whom

showing the Crater, the entire upper rim of which was ascended.

we had known for a few days only, but
there seemed to be no alternative.   Had
he played us false, and made off with the
canoes, we would upon our return to the
beach have been in a very serious predica-

* A point just above the asterisk, where the foot of the
mountain meets the glacier, was the site of our five days' camp.
Directly over this in the illustration is the crater; and the ex·
treme right-hand limit of the upper rim of this — a point about
half an inch to the right of a vertical line drawn from the camp
— was the highest spot reached.

ment. One of the large ones was sent back to Yakutat with seven other Indians, who had accompanied us only as far as Icy Bay. Our native packers carried from seventy to ninety pounds, our white men from sixty to eighty, while my English friends and I had loads varying in weight from twenty-five to forty pounds. We followed the beach in a westerly direction for about five miles. During part of the time we were obliged to walk over ground which was thickly covered with wild strawberries. We found them growing in the sand, of very good size, but somewhat lacking in flavor. The bears are very fond of them, and their tracks may be seen wherever the berries grow.

The route for the first day was substantially that taken by the previous party. We soon left the beach, and turning sharply to the right, followed up one of the many arms of the Yahtsé River, this being the name by which the Jones River is known to the Indians. The Indian name interpreted means " Muddy Harbor River," and it is a very appropriate one. There was no reason why the previous party should have rechristened it, and it is to be hoped that the government will not allow this good old Indian name to be displaced by the name Jones River.

A great deal of wading had to be done through and across the various branches of the Yahtsé, the water of which issued from the glacier less than eight miles beyond, so that its temperature must have been in the neighborhood of 40°. It would be difficult to describe adequately the discomfort caused by entering this cold water, as we were compelled to do on the first day with all our clothes on over twenty times, to depths varying from two to four feet.

The second day out we left the Yahtsé, and ascended the Agassiz Glacier, which lay on our right. This glacier is entirely unlike any we had ever seen. Along its edge and to a height of five hundred feet or more it is so densely wooded with large trees and brush that it is hard for one to realize that a few feet beneath the soil there is solid ice. On emerging from the forest we found ourselves facing an immense moraine, which extended for miles away to the northward and eastward. The Alaskan moraines are different from those commonly seen in Switzerland, which generally consist of stones and bowlders piled up in a continuous line at the edge or on the surface of a glacier. About St. Elias one finds *débris* covering the ice to a greater or lesser depth, and extending quite a distance away from the borders. In the centre of the glacier white ice is generally seen. Travelling over the *débris* is very rough work, and particularly so for men with heavy packs. The stones are loosely distributed, and even with the greatest care in selecting a footing one frequently loses his balance and gets a bad tumble.

Once on the glacier, we were obliged to elect which one of the two routes leading to St. Elias we would take; for before us, at a distance of perhaps eighteen miles, the Chaix Hills, a sandstone range some twelve miles long and thirty-five hundred feet high, lay in such a position that a straight line drawn from us to the mountain would have intersected them at right angles, dividing them into two equal parts. Two years ago the Schwatka party went to the left; and as they expressed the opinion that St. Elias was inaccessible by the face they saw, we decided that it would be better for us to try the other way first.

Most of our Indians had never been on ice before, yet they carried their loads of eighty or ninety pounds over rough and slippery places with comparative ease. More than once we took great pains to cut steps across an ice-slope, to prevent any one from

Mount Crillon from the Pacific Ocean.

slipping ; but they generally disdained using them, crossing either just above or just
below where we had prepared the way.
They refused to wear the shoes with nails
we had provided for them, preferring their
moccasins. Several reached camp one night
with bleeding feet, but they nevertheless
persisted in using their own footgear. We
subsequently discovered that one of their
objects in so doing was to avoid wearing
out good shoes in our service.

The average Indian is a competent being, though it takes some time to discover his good points. He is quick at
grasping ideas, and is especially good at
imitating what others have done. But it
requires great patience in dealing with
him, the more so since he deals with the
white man at arm's length. He is exceedingly distrustful; nor does he cease to be so
until he has become thoroughly convinced
of the honest intentions of the stranger.

In the early part of the third day our
general course was toward the eastern end
of the Chaix Hills; but by noon, our progress being slower than we had anticipated,
we decided to make for the nearest point
on the same, to avoid, if possible, spending
the night on the glacier. We were fortunate in finding a suitable place for leaving the ice. This cannot be done at every
point, owing to the steepness of the glacier at its edge. Between the hills and
the glacier ran a swift stream, after fording
which we found ourselves on a beautiful
camping-ground. The change from the
moraine was very refreshing. To a height
of several hundred feet these hills are
densely wooded with dark green brush;
above grows a kind of coarse grass of a
lighter hue; still higher appear the steep

and bare slopes of sandstone. Pine-trees
are found on a few isolated spots. We
subsequently learned that the northern
face is covered with snow, as might be
expected. It is very odd that such rich
vegetation should be found in the midst
of so much ice.

Eight of the packers were now sent
back to Icy Bay to bring up another supply of food, and two of the Sitka Indians
remained to aid us in moving camp while
exploring the ground that lay before us.
They stayed very reluctantly, and did not
seem to appreciate the distinction we had
intended to confer on them by selecting
them as the two best.

Our immediate object was to reach the
eastern end of the Chaix Hills, by following up the stream, if possible, as walking
along its edge was vastly preferable to crossing the rough glacier. About four miles
above the last camp we discovered a beautiful lake, bordered on one side by the
green hill-slopes, on the other by the steep
cliffs of the glacier. It was only one of a
great number of similar lakes which are to
be found all along this sandstone range.
A flock of ducks rose as we came in sight.
Owing to the steepness of the ice around a
second lake, we were eventually obliged to

take to the glacier again; and by means of it we succeeded, in the course of two days, in turning the hills at the desired point. We were then on a glacier proceeding directly from the southeastern face of the mountain. We ascended it for a short distance, and, from a point about two thousand feet high, obtained a perfect view of the imposing mass of St. Elias, then less than eight miles distant. Though by no means the highest mountain in the world by actual measurement, yet it probably appears as large as, if not larger than, any other; for it is plainly visible from the sea throughout its entire height of about eighteen thousand feet. The Swiss mountains, which are all under sixteen thousand feet, are generally seen from elevations varying from four to eight thousand feet, while in the Himalayas the plane of observation is considerably higher. It is certainly true, that with the possible exception of other peaks in the interior, as yet unknown, Mount St. Elias presents the greatest snow climb in the world, on account of the low point to which the line of perpetual snow descends in these northerly regions. Beside St. Elias such mountains as Cook and Vancouver sank into insignificance. The face we were looking at was composed mainly

Climbing Mount St. Elias

Leaving Yakutat for Icy Bay in Canoes

of great masses of broken snow and ice. On either side were rocky *arêtes* leading up to the final pyramid. The lower part of the mountain seemed much less accessible than the upper part. After a careful survey of the whole, we came to the conclusion that any attempt to make the ascent from that quarter could only result in failure.

In order not to endanger our chances of possible success on the southwestern face through any lack of time, we decided to start for that point at once. This involved retracing our steps to the first place we had reached on the Chaix Hills. A short distance beyond we met the eight packers on their return from Icy Bay; and the party, which then again numbered fourteen, directed their steps to the northwestern corner of the Chaix Hills. Lake Castani, discovered and named by the previous party, happened to be filled with water and floating icebergs as we passed it. On our return, a fortnight later, we found it to be quite empty, the icebergs being stranded. Beyond Castani we were obliged to pass some thick brush before reaching the Guyot Glacier. A walk of three hours over white ice then brought us to the north-western corner of the Chaix Hills.

Just before leaving the glacier, one of our men discovered a large flock of geese on a lake. The whole party was summoned; and, dropping our packs, we armed ourselves with clubs, with a view to having some fresh food for the next meal. The geese were too young to fly; and this was fortunate for us, as we had been obliged to leave all our guns behind, on account of their weight. The geese retired to a sheltered nook beneath a great ice-arch with considerable overhang, which they were only induced to leave on hearing the report of a revolver. As they swam out, a dozen or more were either clubbed or grabbed. We roasted them before an open fire, and found them excellent eating, though doubtless the surrounding circumstances added somewhat to their savor. A fortnight later the geese in the neighborhood were all able to fly, and hence our unsportsmanlike methods ceased to be of any avail.

Our new location on the Chaix Hills was amidst the grandest of mountain scenery. The most conspicuous object was, of course, Mount St. Elias, which rose abruptly from the glacier some twelve miles beyond. Two massive shoulders of snow led up to the summit, in shape re-

sembling a pyramid, three of the edges of
which were visible. Somewhat in advance
of the final peak was what appeared as an
immense crater or amphitheatre, which, if
severed from the rest, would in itself be a
mountain of no mean dimensions. St. Elias
terminates on either side in a long ridge
of as fine precipitous rock as is often seen.
These ridges appear as a continuation of
the shoulders, than which they are, however, so much lower that there is little
difficulty in determining where the mountain proper begins and where it ends.
Turning to the left, the eye, after travel-

Camp at Icy Bay before the start for Mount St. Elias.

ling over immense tracts of glacier, encounters a range of snow-clad mountains with but few protruding rocks. They were particularly beautiful when tinged by the reddish light of the setting sun. In the immediate neighborhood of our camp, violets, forget-me-nots, and bluebells were growing in profusion. A pool of tolerably warm water, fed from subterranean sources, gave us an opportunity of enjoying a delightful swim. It seemed very odd to be bathing when surrounded on all sides by glaciers, and with Mount St. Elias in our immediate vicinity.

Thinking we saw a possible route up the mountain by way of the crater, we decided to move forward immediately. Having crossed the Tyndall Glacier in three hours and a half to Schwatka's last camp on a range of foot-hills, we sent back to Icy Bay all but four of our packers. With them we gradually pushed on up the glacier, and camped the third night after leaving the Chaix Hills near the mouth of the second of the three glaciers which join the Tyndall on the left and at right angles. At this point one of the party had the misfortune to meet with an accident which rendered it inadvisable for him to attempt any further climbing. Leaving him and the two Indians at the camp last mentioned, the remaining three of us, with two white packers, pushed right on to the base of the mountain and crater, and pitched our tent on the only green spot on the southwestern face of St. Elias.

This spot, covering perhaps two acres, was about three thousand feet above the level of the sea, on what may be said to represent the line of perpetual snow on Mount St. Elias. We had some little trouble in reaching it, owing to the treacherous condition of the glacier up which we were obliged to proceed. The latter is very much crevassed for a distance of two miles or more from the mountain. In the very early part of the season it is probably covered with so much snow that one would hardly become aware of the presence of the ice beneath; but by the end of July much of the snow has disappeared; and the remaining snow-bridges over the crevasses, being then very thin, are liable to break when subjected to any great pressure. Hence we had to feel our way along very carefully, and at times retrace our steps for a considerable distance in order to try getting ahead at another point. As we were tied together with a stout rope, which was kept taut when in dangerous places, the

only result following the breaking through
of a snow-bridge was the temporary dis-
appearance, partial or total, of one of the
party beneath the snow. With the aid
of the rope he was able to regain the surface with little or no trouble. Without
the rope, though, a person would in many
cases fall to a great depth, where he would
be jammed in the ice or freeze to death
before any assistance could be rendered.
Of course it is of the utmost importance
that crevasses which are hidden by snow
should be crossed at right angles; for if
several are on a snow-bridge at once, and
it breaks through, the rope ceases to be of
any avail, and all may come to grief. Such
accidents, however, need not occur when
proper care is exercised in examining the
surface of the snow.

Our party was the first to set foot on
Mount St. Elias; for the previous expedition, having proceeded up the Tyndall
Glacier to within a certain distance of the
mountain, decided to branch off to the
left on account of the roughness of the ice
ahead.*   Mr. Karr then ascended, to a
height of about seven thousand feet, one of
a chain of hills which faces the main range,
but constitutes in no sense any part of it.

* Karr's " Shores and Alps of Alaska," p. 102.   Schwatka's
letter to the *New York Times*, Oct. 7, 1886.

Heretofore the fuel question had never given us any trouble, as we had always succeeded in finding wood or brush wherever we had stopped; but now our fires were comparatively small, being fed only by bits of shrubbery and dry moss. We were, however, always able to boil enough water for coffee; and no further cooking was required, as we had, in anticipation of finding no fuel on the mountain, brought with us boiled hams and hard tack for use while there.

The view from our camping-ground was one of rare beauty. A small portion of the summit of Mount St. Elias was visible, peeping up over the crater. Its great

Wading an arm of the Yahtse River on the return from the Mountain.

Mount La Pérouse and the

height, however, could not be fully appreciated from so near its base. A most remarkable and unique sight were two straight and narrow glaciers, which appeared to have fallen over the edge of the mountain at a point where it was very steep. They were parallel, and were separated by a strip of fine bare rock. They resembled two frozen cascades, and must have been over two thousand feet high. For the first time we caught a glimpse of the valley through which the upper part of the Tyndall Glacier descends. The

Great Pacific Glacier, from the Ocean.

rocky peaks and precipices in the background were very grand, reminding us
somewhat of the scenery from Montan-
vert looking up the Mer de Glace.

No less than fourteen different kinds of
wild-flowers were found near our camp,
and a few excellent strawberries were
picked.   Ptarmigan, which during the
last few days had been seen in large numbers, had now grown scarce, though with
the aid of a gun we could have secured
enough for several meals.   Four marmots
were captured by smoking them out of

their hole in the cleft of a rock. Situated as we were, they made an excellent stew, to prepare which we destroyed one of our wooden boxes. Two bears were seen crossing the glacier. They did not trouble us, and we had no means of troubling them.

From our camp on the mountain the crater was reached by two different *arêtes* and on two different occasions. The ascent alone of the first *arête* occupied the better part of eight hours, and was not free from difficulty. The height reached was about eight thousand feet. A low, broad cairn was built at the top. Being of the opinion that the route we had chosen was too long for the beginning of the ascent of such a mountain as St. Elias, we decided to ascertain whether the crater could not be gained more easily in some other way. The night previous to the second successful attempt to reach it was spent in the open air, two hours beyond the regular camp, at a somewhat chilly spot. We were surrounded on almost every side by snow and ice, so we could hardly expect very much warmth after the sun had gone down. The glacier to the left of us was very peculiar. It seemed to have its origin in a rocky precipice, and consisted mainly of yawning crevasses. It was evidently the remnant of a once fine glacier coming down from above.

A start was made at 4.30 A.M. The Tophams and I were tied to a rope, our two packers remaining at the base of the mountain. After two hours and a half of steady climbing we had gained the crater by a rock *arête* running parallel to the one we had already ascended. Our experience with the rocks of Mount St. Elias was not of an agreeable character. They were practically all composed of shale of the most rotten kind, thus affording no hold for either our hands or our feet. Large pieces broke off and went tumbling down below at every step we took, filling the air with dust; and at times we were obliged to use great care in order to avoid going along with them. Had the rock been firm, the climbing would have been very fine, as the *arête* was quite rugged. The sharp character of the shale was most injurious to our shoes, however stout they were; and the integrity of our footgear was, of course, a question of the utmost importance to us.

Once on the brink of the crater, we obtained a perfect view of this wonderful cavity in the mountain-side. It is one of the main features of the southwestern face

of St. Elias.   It begins on the right in a
splendid jagged *arête* leading up to a peak
which, from another point, appears as a
spur of the mountain.   At the foot of this
peak begins the upper rim of the crater,
which descends gradually to the left in the
shape of a spiral curve.   In its entire length
it is frosted with a layer of snow over fifty
feet thick, the effect of which is very
striking.   The walls of the crater are composed of steep, bare rock, the surface of
which is furrowed and stratified in a most
wonderful manner.   The interior is filled
with snow; its outlet being to the eastward, where it feeds a large glacier.   There
is some reason for believing that this amphitheatre is of volcanic origin.   Several
specimens of rocks which were brought
down seem to support this theory, while
later in the day a cone was passed resembling in shape and general appearance those
seen in the crater of Kilauea, on the island
of Hawaii.

Having paused a few moments for the
view, we turned to the left, and began following the edge of the crater in a westerly
direction.   We soon passed the point we
had reached two days before, and then
walked steadily for two hours over snow-
fields and steep *débris*.   Later we had about

fifteen minutes of good climbing among solid sandstone and conglomerate rocks, which we enjoyed immensely, as it was in marked contrast with what we had been treated to on the shale *arête*.

After a hasty lunch at ten we continued the ascent. The following hour was occupied in cutting our way up an ice-slope. This is always slow and tedious work, and particularly so when the ice is covered with a layer of snow. At an early hour of the day such slopes can sometimes be ascended by digging one's feet into the snow, and without the aid of any steps in the ice; but after the surface has been exposed to the rays of the sun, there is always danger of the whole mass of snow detaching itself from the ice, and forming a miniature avalanche; in which case the whole party would be pretty sure to follow the avalanche down the slope. It is far safer, and generally absolutely necessary, when brought face to face with such an obstacle, to cut one's way up it step by step. The rate of progress under such circumstances is often not over a hundred and fifty feet an hour, whereas a good snow-field can be climbed at more than ten times this speed. The steps are cut by means of an ice-axe, the shape of which is familiar to Swiss tourists. The first man has most of the heavy work to do. Those behind him have to see that the rope is kept taut, and to dig their axes well into the ice at each step, in order to have a good hold, should any one slip. The descent of such a slope is generally accomplished in the same way that one would descend a ladder. When thus facing the ice, there is less danger of losing one's balance. Then, too, it is easier to secure a foothold in a slippery step with the toe than with the heel.

Having climbed the ice-slope, we found ourselves at the point where the crater appears from below to take a sudden turn to the right. We then walked along the undulating line of its upper edge. No sooner had we reached the top of one eminence than we were obliged to descend again, only to prepare for climbing another. The snow was very soft, and we constantly went in to our knees and sometimes to our waist. At 1.45 P.M. we were at the point where the rocky peak already referred to may properly be said to begin. According to observations made with aneroid barometers and a boiling-point thermometer, the height reached was 11,460 feet, nearly 9,000 of which were above the line of perpetual snow. Several sights were taken with the prismatic compass, in order to locate our position on the mountain. It was unfortunately too late in the day, and the snow was getting too soft, for us to ascend the small peak. We estimated it to be about 1,500 feet above us, and under favorable conditions could probably have climbed it in less than two hours.

There are several reasons, which it would be tedious for the reader to have laid before him at length, why no further attempt was made to reach the actual summit of Mount St. Elias. The only practicable route leading to the final peak from beyond the crater appeared to be over a huge mound some 1,500 feet high, the slopes of which were mostly covered with ice. To cut steps up it would in itself be no small task, and would have to be performed at the beginning, and not in the middle, of the day's climb: hence it would be necessary to establish a temporary camp at a considerable height on the mountain; and to do this would require the services of packers experienced in climbing, such as the present expedition did not have at its command. Even then success would not be certain, unless another year should find these same slopes covered with firm snow instead of ice. That this would be the

case is not at all improbable, in view of the
unusual amount of sunny weather which
prevailed in Alaska during the whole of the
summer of 1888, the tendency of which is
to turn snow into ice. Beyond the mound
the ascent by the southern *arête* appeared
to offer fewer difficulties, though the very
summit of the mountain wore a snowcap
with a great deal of overhang. The southwestern face of St. Elias, it is safe to say,
will never be climbed. It presents a mass
of broken snow, beautiful yet forbidding.
We estimated the summit to be about
7,000 feet above us, making its total height
18,500 feet. It seemed to us that the Coast
Survey, giving it 19,500 feet, was too lib-
eral in its figures.*

The day was cloudless. The whole
scene was one that baffles description. It
surpassed in grandeur, though not in pic-
turesqueness, the very best that the Alps can
offer. Roughly speaking, the eye encountered for miles nothing but snow and ice.
I had never before thoroughly realized the
vastness of the Alaskan glaciers, though
during the past fortnight we had spent
many a weary hour in crossing immense

---

* NOTE. — In 1891, two years after the writing of the above,
the height of Mount St. Elias was determined to be 18,100 feet,
which measurement is now adopted by the Government. — ED.

moraines. One of the glaciers we looked down upon was not less than sixty miles long, while another attained a breadth of twenty-five or thirty miles.

From below I had gained the impression that ice covered with *débris* predominated over white ice. I now saw that this was not the case, and that the ratio of *débris* to clear ice was probably not greater than that of one to ten. When standing at a considerable height, one appreciates for the first time the beautiful curves through which the glaciers alter their courses. We noticed this in particular in looking down upon the Agassiz Glacier. It appeared at one point to describe three or four arcs of concentric circles with radii varying from eight to ten miles, each arc being indicated by a light coating of stones, the whole resembling an immense race-course. Through the middle of the Tyndall Glacier, and for a distance of several miles, two light streaks of moraine ran parallel to each other, presenting from above the appearance of a huge serpent crawling the length of the glacier.

The groups of snow-clad peaks visible to the naked eye were countless; and to the northward, in which direction the view was barred, their number is doubtless quite as great. Only a few of them, however, impressed us as being either very high, or very striking in shape. Some of them rose out of the snow in such a manner as to lead one to believe that they had been recently buried, and were waiting to be dug out. When I say that but few appeared very high or striking, I should except Fair-weather and Crillon, which towered above the clouds, though a hundred and forty miles distant. The ocean was covered with fog, as it frequently is in these latitudes. In fact, it would often be raining for a whole day at the beach, while about St. Elias the sky would be cloudless.

At three o'clock we thought it best to begin our downward journey, as we did not care to be caught out over night without blankets. A small American flag, presented to the expedition by a lady of Sitka, was placed in a tin can and left at "Flag Rock," a point about ten thousand feet high. The descent was accomplished without accident, and we reached our sleeping-place at 8.30 P.M. While descending the final *arête*, and when not occupied in dodging falling stones, we noticed some very fine effects of the setting sun on the snow mountains and on a few thin floating clouds. The hues did not equal the Alpine glow of Switzerland, but the light blue of the sky was very beautiful. The sunlight falling on the green spots in the valleys below made them stand out in marked contrast with the surrounding snow and ice.

After a hasty meal we wrapped ourselves up in our blankets, and spent another night in the open air. We had all enjoyed the day thoroughly. I shall certainly remember it as one of the pleasantest I have ever spent in the mountains.

The twentieth day had now elapsed since our arrival at Icy Bay; and it was time for us to be thinking of getting back to the beach, not knowing how long we might be detained there by the surf. Leaving a few things behind, we began the return journey in earnest the day after the climb, and reached the shore in the course of five days. The Indians were overjoyed at the idea of being homeward bound. They seemed thoroughly tired of the mountains. We found the Yahtsé River very much higher than when we had come up, and hence the wading was more disagreeable. At one place we were submerged for some time anywhere from the chest to the neck, according to the size of the man. We were so light when under water, that the quicksands below did not trouble us. On the other hand, our loads rendered us top-heavy; and one of our men, as a natural result, lost his balance, and went over, wetting his pack. Our smallest Indian had to be relieved of his load altogether. Curiously enough, the Indians seemed to prefer wading to walking over dry ground. The first day out they took us through deep and cold water no less than ten times in the course of half an hour, part of which could have been avoided, as we subsequently found, by making a short *détour* through the woods. On the present occasion one of them, having crossed the stream, deposited his pack, and returned to the deepest part, where he literally took a bath with all his clothes on, and seemed to rejoice in our unsuccessful efforts at finding a shallow place for crossing. The water, coming directly from the glacier, was so cold that we white men were only too glad to get out of it; but its temperature seemed to have no disagreeable effect on the Indians.

The shore-camp was reached Aug. 7, early in the afternoon. There was but little surf; and fearing that the conditions might change by next morning, we decided to start for Yakutat that night. The Indians were very glad to leave, and as a consequence we found getting away from

A Rainy Day on the March to the Mountain.

Icy Bay to be a very much easier task than starting out from Yakutat some four weeks earlier had been. The large canoe carried twelve men, all the baggage, and the provisions which were left over. The small one could only hold four men. At six o'clock we were fairly under way, and an equal amount of paddling and sailing brought us to Yakutat next morning at ten o'clock.

Four days elapsed, and the Alpha, which we were relying on to take us down the coast, had not yet put in an appearance. As I was anxious to be in New York by October, I availed myself of an unexpected opportunity to reach Sitka on the Active, a small schooner which was already crowded with miners. My friends, not being so hard pressed for time, decided to await the arrival of the larger vessel. The Active was favored with a fair breeze till within thirty miles of Sitka, at which point we took to the oars, and rowed her into port at the rate of about two miles an hour. The trip was performed in three days and a half, and, thanks to the fine weather, was far from disagreeable, notwithstanding the very primitive character of the accommodations.

The others were, as I subsequently learned, much less fortunate than myself in getting away from Yakutat. After waiting another week for the Alpha, one of them decided to start for Sitka in a canoe with some Indians. The trip was successfully made in seven days; but it was a dangerous one to attempt, since the coast consists largely of rocks and glaciers, and hence offers but little protection against southerly gales, even for a canoe. On reaching Sitka it was learned that the Leo, a schooner with auxiliary steam-power, was just about to leave for Victoria. She was immediately chartered to go to Yakutat, and bring the remainder of the party away. Their joy on sighting her was intense, but not of long duration; for no sooner had she steamed off with all on board, than a south-easterly gale was encountered, which lasted five days. During this time the Leo sprung a bad leak, which necessitated a return to Yakutat, where she was beached and repaired by her crew. Sitka was eventually reached on the 17th of September.

It is hoped that before long this part of our country will be visited again, and another attempt made to climb Mount St. Elias. The next expedition will have a great advantage over the present one; for, the weather permitting, it can count on being at an elevation of eleven thousand four hundred feet above the sea-level within six days after leaving Icy Bay, whereas this year's party were eighteen days in reaching this height, owing to the absence of all definite information concerning the mountain proper.

Whether the latter will ever be climbed by following up our route it is impossible to say. It is not at all unlikely that the true way to the summit is to be found on the northern side, where fewer rocks and better snow would probably be encountered. How to reach the northern side of the mountain is a problem yet to be solved. But whether successful in reaching the top or not, no party composed of men who enjoy walking and climbing amidst the finest of alpine scenery will ever regret having spent a summer in making the attempt to ascend Mount St. Elias.

Since the writing of the foregoing article two further attempts have been made to ascend Mount St. Elias; one in 1890, and the other in 1891. They were made under the joint auspices of the United States Geological Survey Department and the

National Geographical Society; and both expeditions were in charge of Mr. I. C. Russell, now a professor of Ann Arbor University. These attempts were made on the northern side of the mountain. On the first a height of about 10,000 feet was reached, and on the second a height of 14,500 feet. Descriptions of them by Mr. Russell will be found in the *Century Magazine* for April, 1891, and June, 1892, and an account of the first one by Mr. M. B. Kerr on page 275 of this volume. One of the results of the first expedition was the announcement (which was indeed startling to the members of the expedition which I had joined), that the height of the mountain was only 15,200 feet. In 1891 this error was, however, corrected, and the height fixed at 18,100 feet, plus or minus a probable error of one hundred feet. This latest measurement substantially confirms the rough estimate of the height assigned to the mountain by my party in 1888.

Since 1891 no further attempt has been made to climb Mount St. Elias. This is not surprising when it is remembered that the undertaking is very costly, both as regards time and money, while the result must always be uncertain. If the same climbing facilities existed in the neighborhood of this mountain as exist at the very foot, so to speak, of each prominent peak of the Alps, — i.e., if hotels, provisions, and guides were found within two or three days' march of the summit of Mount St. Elias, — the latter would doubtless be ascended from the northern side with no greater difficulty than attends the ascent of first-class snow-peaks in Switzerland. In other words, the mountaineering difficulties presented by this great Alaskan peak are, standing alone, probably not of an extraordinary character ; but these difficulties in combination with those arising out

Mount St. Elias, from Yakutat.

of the location of the mountain, far away from any civilized settlement, and in the midst of rough glaciers of immense extent, across which all provisions and equipment must be carried or dragged by human agency before an opportunity to do any real climbing presents itself, render the matter of the ascent quite a serious problem, the solution of which should not be entered upon lightly.

MOUNT ST. ELIAS

AND ITS GLACIERS

By Mark Brickell Kerr

The First Climb.

INCE 1741, when Bering,
in the course of his great
voyage, discovered St. Elias,
and named this grand
mountain-peak after the
patron saint of the day,
many voyagers and explorers have turned
their thoughts and energy to accurately
determine its correct height and true position. Captain Cook, about 1778; La
Pérouse, about 1787; and, later, Malaspina, whose unrequited services and death
in a Spanish prison rival the experiences
of Columbus in the ingratitude of human-
ity; Vancouver, in 1794; and many Russian

275

navigators,— Ismaleff, Berchareff, and Teb-
enkoff, — all saw St. Elias, and most of
them took sextant observations for its altitude and position.

The elevation generally adopted until
1874 was that placed upon the British
Admiralty charts; viz., 14,970 feet. In
that year a party of the United States
Coast and Geodetic Survey made a reconnoissance of Mount St. Elias and vicinity,
and obtained results for altitude and position by means of open triangles with long
sides. This placed the height at 19,500
feet, and was adopted by geographers as
the best evidence extant for altitude. Since
then three expeditions have been sent to
climb the mountain, one in 1886, under
Lieutenant Schwatka, called the *New York
Times* Expedition, and another, in 1888,
under Harold Topham, of the Royal Geographical Society and English Alpine Club.
Both these attempts failed, as the ascent
was tried from the south, or ocean, side,
where the crystalline slopes are almost perpendicular. The latter party, by aneroid,
reached an elevation of 11,000 feet. A
sketch of this expedition, by Mr. William
Williams, one of the party, is to be found
on page 225 of the present volume.

The third party was sent out in June,

1890, by the National Geographic Society, in command of I. C. Russell, geologist. To this party the writer was attached, in charge of the geographic work of the expedition. It is the narrative of the journey of this party which I have to detail. The work of this expedition places St. Elias at 15,350 feet,* agreeing fairly well with former determinations by Malaspina and other navigators of the last century. Mount Cook is 12,370, and Mount Vancouver 9,884 feet.

Taking advantage of the experience of former expeditions, our party made the attempt from the head of Yakutat Bay, and on the eastern face of the mountain.

For many years public interest has centred around the most remote of our possessions, and many are the tales related of the wonders of Alaskan scenery. Examining all the data extant to-day, very little is found outside the beaten tracks, — that is, those portions where the tourist steamers yearly go. If you look in an ordinary gazetteer, you will find that Alaska covers about five hundred and eighty thousand square miles, is rich in minerals and fur-

---

* Careful recalculation of the results of 1890 gave 16,700 feet, and other points higher proportionally.

bearing animals, has large fishing interests, immense snowy peaks, and huge glaciers. The charts show its coast-line in a general way, but the interior is almost a blank. This lack of definite knowledge was the reason our party was organized, particularly to explore the vicinity of St. Elias, determine its altitude, and ascend it if practicable.

We outfitted at Seattle, Wash., and hired seven stalwart woodsmen, who seemed particularly well adapted for our work, and rendered us independent of Indian packers, who have been found so unreliable in former expeditions. Our provisions were carefully selected, and placed in tins of convenient size for protection against rain and flood (ten days' rations for one man in each tin), and we were extremely thankful afterward that we used such precautions.

I will pass lightly over the events of our journey to Sitka, through the inland narrows which have been so ably described by others. We were fortunate in securing passage on the Queen with Captain Carroll, whose pleasant and cordial treatment did much to make the journey enjoyable; and his knowledge of the country assisted us greatly. We passed Wrangel, the Narrows, Douglas Island, Juneau, and arrived at Glacier Bay on June 23. At first sight the Muir Glacier was disappointing, my imagination having pictured a more magnificent field of ice ; but on climbing a little hill, I soon beheld the extensive *névé*, the rocky islets and long moraines extending twelve or fifteen miles northward, the regular and beautiful curves only limited by the surrounding peaks, whose summits rose above the intervening fleecy clouds. At noon the mist cleared, and our sail out of Glacier Bay will long be remembered as one of the most delightful in my experience. Some bergs of ice floating majestically, with their different forms, and hues varying from deep azure to pale blue, mingled with others where the morainal material had changed the color to a dark brown. Very skilful manœuvring was required to take the vessel through these masses of floating ice, and many were the comments on the splendid seamanship of our skipper. Here, in the crisp morning air, we had a fine view of the Fairweather group, uplifting their snowy crests, a barrier to the scene eastward. The immense fields of ice and snow made us shudder, even from our great distance, as we thought of crossing them ; and we turned with pleasure to the comfortable surroundings of our good ship.

We arrived at Sitka early on the morning of June 24, and after arranging every detail with Governor Knapp and the naval authorities, transferred our stores to the United States steamer Pinta ; and Captain Farenhalt, U. S. Navy, made everything ready to start for Yakutat Bay early the next morning.

We entered Yakutat Bay June 26, anchoring off the Indian village ; but during our stay there it rained continuously, and we did not even catch a glimpse of St. Elias, much to our regret.

On the morning of June 28 we started up the bay, Lieutenant Karl Jungen, U.S. Navy, and myself leading in the whale-boat, followed by our flotilla of canoes. We secured the Moravian missionary at Mulgrave, Mr. Hendrickson, for guide ; and he also afterward read my barometer at the Mission, giving a reference-point for all barometric observations.

In the afternoon the Pinta's boats, after giving us three cheers, left to rejoin the ship ; and we turned to in the rain to make ourselves as comfortable as possible, realizing that our work had begun in sober earnest. At this juncture my assistant, Mr. Edward Hosmer of Washington, who had been quite sick for a few days, was taken

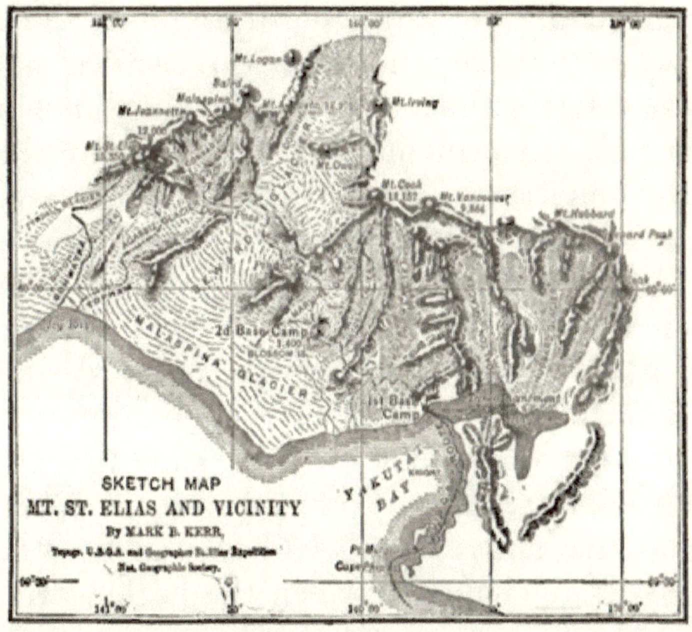

so ill that he was obliged to return to Mulgrave village, and thence to Sitka. Our party then consisted of Israel C. Russell, geologist; Mark B. Kerr, topographer; J. H. Christie, foreman; and Lester Doney, William Partridge, Jack Crumback, William L. Lindsly, Tom White, and Tom Stamy, woodsmen.

On the 29th, with two men and a load of stores, I started ahead, and the next day succeeded in landing on the north shore of Yakutat Bay, great care being used to avoid the masses of ice which, breaking off from the Hubbard and Dalton Glaciers above us, crunched and grounded here on the beach, threatening to destroy our frail canoe. The bay narrows here to about three miles, and opens farther inland into another one known as Disenchantment Bay. Looking up the bay, one sees a verdure-ciad shore, above which rises a vertical wall of ice fully three hundred feet, the end of the Hubbard Glacier, over which tower the great snowy peaks, Vancouver, Hubbard, Shepard, and Bozman. Here I had a lesson in surf-landing; but it took me some time to learn a trick so readily accomplished by even the smallest native boys. They usually wait for a fair chance between the high waves, and then rush in, and the canoe is quickly hauled up out of reach of the surf. Many were the duckings we had before this could be done in safety.

I had my first experience in the snow on July 3, and was greatly surprised to find it lying so low down on the slope. The snow-line here is about one thousand five hundred feet above the sea, and is as clearly marked as in the Sierras of California. Moss, shrubs, and berries grew in great profusion along the bay shore, and over the moraine a regular trail was formed as the large brown bears crossed and re-crossed in search of food or berries. The glacial stream divided into a thousand branches, and formed an ideal delta, depositing silt and glacial *débris*. Our course took us over a mountain spur, and across an interior basin about one thousand five hundred feet in height, filled with numerous lakes, and swarming with mosquitoes. Indeed, there were such myriads of the latter that imagination suggested that each flake of snow had concealed within it a germ, and thus the mosquito had generated. Here it is said that sometimes huge brown bears, driven to fury and desperation by these tormenting little beasts, finally tear their flesh, and die in agony. This was the first high ridge we crossed with our packs, and very glad were we to view the other side.

Our course took us to the head of Dalton River, where a curious phenomenon was observed. The water was flowing out of an icy cavern, above which was a stratum of ice, rock, and dirt, on the surface of which bushes and trees were growing. This formation was gradually caving in, and borne by the stream to the sea. The same phenomenon was seen at Styx River, farther on, across the Lucia Glacier.

Crevasses were wide and deep, cutting the ice in fantastic shapes. We advanced slowly during the next three weeks, absolutely feeling our way over the rough moraines; two miles a day was heavy travelling, and it took several trips to bring up all our camp outfit and tins of provisions. The rocks tore our shoe-leather and cut our feet, and human endurance was exerted to the utmost to force our way over this rough and icy glacier.

Happily sufficient vegetation was found on the lower slopes to afford fuel. We crossed several swift and icy-cold streams, and numerous curious holes or kettles in the glacier, where great care was necessary, as a single misstep meant a fall of many hundred feet.

On July 25 I went ahead with one man, to prospect the Kettle Cañon and the Hayden Glacier. We took an oil-stove and a small outfit, and even then we had to carry about forty or fifty pounds each. At the head of this cañon, Hayden Glacier has a width of two miles. Across the glacier, a point of the ridge came down covered with spruce-trees. Flowers, grasses, and ferns were growing luxuriantly around me; and as I rested in the soft moss, and looked over a cathedral mass of rock from a lupine bed of beautiful colors, I seemed to breathe the atmosphere of the Tropics, rather than of the Arctic.

Head of the Dalton River — water flowing from an icy cavern.

The Hayden—the third glacier of great importance on our route—begins with a surface of hard ice about two or three miles in width, and gradually ends in a huge moraine of dirt, rocks, and ice, belching its contents into Yakutat Bay. As you proceed up the glacier, the slopes on both sides become perpendicular. Huge massive slate and sandstone ridges rise up on both sides, clear-cut and defined, with niches like an open fan. After a few miles, the upper level is reached; and then the journey is made through soft snow, sinking in over boot-tops at every step, and progress is slow and difficult.

Toward evening of the 25th we had reached an elevation of twenty-five hundred feet, and here found a slope with a few loose rocks deposited at an angle of about thirty degrees. We riprapped the bottom of the slope to prevent slipping down the hill, and here made camp. All around was a snowy expanse broken into curious shapes, with nothing living except a raven, which suddenly and hoarsely croaked above our heads. I felt like offering the bird an apology for being there.

The next day we tried two points of the ridge, but could not cross over on account of the crevasses. However, we found a more desirable point of rock upon which to pitch camp. The day after, in a fog, we went up toward the last promising pass, and at the top of the divide were met by a *berg schründer*, which stretched across the slope about six to ten feet wide, and about five hundred feet in depth. The walls of these crevasses were laminated; and each year's snow was easily discerned by its difference in color, radiating like the rings of a tree.

As I looked into the depths of the crevasse, I grew bewildered in endeavoring to discover its age, and pictured to myself the time when almost the whole world was an ice-field, grinding and twisting out forms so familiar to us at places where now one could scarcely believe the ice had ever formed. Here, on the extreme summit of one of these sandstone ridges, I discovered a hill of fossil mussel-shells, and also ferns and flowers, embedded in the rock, evidences of a great ocean once rolling over these rock masses. The fog still continued; and as I lay in my rocky perch, protected from the pelting rain by only a canvas sheet, I was suddenly startled by a dreadful report, as an avalanche of ice and rock, detached by the rain, came thundering down the mountain slope. These immense ice-fields, split up by huge crevasses, assume all sorts of shapes. Combining the shadows and effects of the surrounding patches of massive rock left here and there, imagination runs riot. I could see a picture where white-robed choristers and surpliced priests passed in endless file, while the huge black masses of shaly rock of the higher peaks stood out like the spires of a mighty cathedral, the lower slopes, the pipes of an immense organ, to which picture the thunder of the avalanche supplied the deep diapason.

On the 28th, after a hard struggle, we succeeded in reaching the summit of the pass, and were rewarded by a few hours of clear weather. St. Elias, Augusta, and Cook burst upon us in all their glory, rivalling anything I had ever before seen. Here were deep crevasses, high domes, hummocks, and bergs of ice, and above towered the huge peaks, sharp and steep. But soon the fog arose, and we were forced to return. We spent a most miserable and wet night. In the very early morning, as the rain gradually loosened the rocky and icy *débris*, and the pieces went whizzing by, threatening to ingulf us, we were forced to move out. It was a rough trip; but we reached Kettle Cañon, wet to the skin, and found the main camp moved ahead to Blossom Island, where we spent the next few days in examining the ice formations and extending triangulation.

This was an oasis in a desert of surrounding ice, — the last point where we found wood, and a most beautiful spot, completely environed by a glacial stream. The flora here was abundant and varied. Lupines of all colors, bluebells, and ferns of every description flourished in rank profusion;

Mount St. Elias and its Glaciers
Lucia Glacier

while clusters of wild currants and salmon-berries grew in immense quantities, the latter, especially, to an enormous size, in this damp but equable temperature. Indeed, the thermometer scarcely varied during the day more than five degrees from an average of fifty degrees, but the rain was heavy and continuous. During the night the thermometer fell, sometimes reaching freezing-point. In the winter the temperature falls to just below freezing-point; and this rain, converted into snow, piles up in immense quantities.

A few bumble-bees and house-flies were noted; and the mosquito still held its own, rendering a trip through the thickets and underbrush almost an impossibility. There were quite a number of ptarmigan and whistling marmots; and, although signs of bear were numerous, we saw none. From this, our last point of vegetation, we decided to start a reconnoissance trip to explore the route toward St. Elias and Cook, now in full view from our camp at the summit of Blossom Island.

On Aug. 2 we started up the glacier, which we named "Marvine," and camped, during a storm of rain, on a ledge of rock at an elevation of twenty-five hundred feet above the sea. We passed a very disagreeable night. The rain continued loosening the rocks and *débris* above us; and soon these came whizzing by, too close for comfort. When one large rock struck my alpenstock, which was used for a tent-pole, and diverted its course just enough to miss cracking open my skull, I thought we had best move camp; so down in the snow we moved, through the rain, and spent the rest of the night huddled over an oil-stove, and enjoyed a good cup of coffee, brewed at the early hour of three A.M.

The next day we found a very comfort-able camping-place in hard snow, which we covered with dirt and rocks from the moraine. The grade ahead seemed easy; but a storm again beginning, we took shel-ter in an ice grotto, where the drippings from the roof gave us delicious drinking-water, and rendered our hard-tack and cold bacon more palatable. The crevasses here are clean-cut, deep, and without much ornamentation; and the ice, of a dark blue, gives a rather subdued effect.

The next morning the sun shone out strong and warm; and the rays dancing over the surface of the crystallized snow glittered like clusters of diamonds, and soon put new life and vigor into our half-frozen limbs. We moved over Pinnacle

Pass at an elevation of 4,200 feet. From here we could see the black ridges and lower points of the Rogers Range; while a large glacier extended in front, and turned northward out of our sight. We named it the "Seward." It was the largest we had seen, and cut up and crevassed in curves like ribbons of watered silk. The day was clear; and the huge glacier was seen to slope seaward in gentle, undulating curves, — a peaceful, icy river, broken only by its fall into the Malaspina Glacier. It looked so much like the sea that one of our men exclaimed, "Look at the ocean!" But between us and the sea extended the mighty Malaspina Glacier, which covers the whole side of Yakutat Bay. We made our camp for the night under a sandstone ledge, where the water was flowing over the old ice. It may seem strange to hear of our hunting for water in this land of ice; but the cascades, formed away up on the slopes, plunge down huge crevasses, and disappear under the snowy bed. Sometimes we were forced to use our small supply of oil to melt the snow for the water needed in our cooking. Our camp was on the east side of the Seward Glacier, which extended far northward to the base of the main range. St. Elias — silent, massive, dark, rugged, and sharp — lay right in front, while Augusta stood like an immense haystack, a gable, on the right; the snow banners floating quietly by, covering and uncovering these beautiful and grand mountains fully ten thousand feet above us. We held our breath in silent awe, and wondered at our audacity in attempting to scale the dizzy heights.

The Seward Glacier is a natural divide between the ridge through which we had forced our way and the main range. So one part of the problem was solved, and

View of Mount Cook and the Seward Glacier.

we discovered that there was no main range parallel to the coast; while angulation determined another point, and that was that the elevation had been very much over-estimated, and St. Elias was much lower than 19,500 feet. The ranges are all broken by immense faults, and it was owing to such structure that Pinnacle Pass was found so easy of passage.

We moved slowly along, loud reports resounding on all sides; and avalanches rushed down as the sun gradually melted the snow. Keeping well out into the middle of the glacier, we felt safe. Soon, however, we were forced by the rough ice and crevasses to the side of the glacier, and, climbing a ridge, our farther progress seemed barred; so we camped on a ledge about one hundred feet above the ice, with just room enough to pitch our 7×7 tent, into which we four men crawled, — a sardine pack truly. The glacier groaned, the ice crunched, and huge pieces fell in here and there with a loud noise, as the pressure from above was felt. There was more perceptible movement here than in any other glacier. We estimated it at about fifteen feet a day. The Seward Glacier is limited by a range on the north, the highest point of which we named Logan,* in honor of the late Director of the Geological Survey of Canada.

The blocks of ice here were like huge Christmas cakes, and often during the night we could actually feel the glacier move. And when the rain came pelting down, and the wind blew furiously, and pieces of ice toppled over with a noise like a pistol-shot, we wondered when we would again be out of danger.

Two of our men had gone back for provisions, and on the 17th we became a little anxious about them. The sunset on this night was superb. The shadows began to lengthen, and the huge peaks reflected their long summits on the snowy surface like enormous arms. To the west stretched the main breadth of the glacier, fully ten miles across, with many branches cut up by concave crevasses, which, though twisted and irregular, were connected by small bridges of snow, sometimes scarcely a foot in width; all followed a regular curve of cleavage caused by the contraction of the ice, the strain, and subsequent movement.

The peaks of the Yakutat Bay spurs, and the point of Cook, presented their

* The United States Coast and Geodetic Survey Expedition of 1892 accurately measured Mount Logan, and found it 19,500 feet, the highest peak of the St. Elias range.

sharpest angles toward us, and the sandstone cliffs standing above the snow could easily be mistaken for volcanic dikes. We could readily understand how St. Elias, Cook, and other peaks of the range presenting to the sea their upturned angular strata, and consequently sharpest, steepest slopes, have been mistaken for volcanoes. It was bewildering to watch these snowfields, which in the setting sun were not luminous, but a fine, clear, white expanse, gradually assuming a darker hue as the sun gradually dropped behind St. Elias.

We smiled to think of the great care taken by Alpine guides, forbidding even a whisper upon the Mer de Glace, or a journey without a guide upon the glacier. If such a mountaineer were suddenly transported to the great Seward Glacier, and felt the glacier tremble, and listened to the constantly falling avalanches from the crags of Elias and Cook, I imagine he would throw away his alpenstock, and flee in dismay.

On the 18th of August, our men having returned with oil and provisions, we moved directly toward Mount St. Elias. I blacked my face, and wore netting and heavy goggles, as the glare from the ice was terrific. We crossed the Dome Pass, leading over into the Agassiz Glacier; and, looking ahead, the route seemed blocked by crevasses and ice-falls. This was the glacier discovered by Schwatka and Seton Karr; but they were not aware of its extent. It was slow work clambering through the crevasses, heading some and cutting our way through others; but with care we reached the first ice-fall about noon. Here we were forced to cut steps in the ice, but after reaching the summit were turned back by a huge crevasse. Finally we cut our way down into it until it was narrow enough to straddle; and we then gradually cut our way up on the opposite side, the first man being lowered by a rope. Great care was used; for if a slip occurred, a man might lose his life, or be frightfully maimed, these crevasses often being over five hundred feet in depth.

Afterward we were forced to the centre of the glacier, and had fairly good travelling until we reached the second ice-fall. Here we found an opening through which a stream was flowing over the old and hard ice, but with a gentle current, not enough to impede us. We waded along this, knee-deep, until every bone in our bodies seemed frozen; and we were obliged to camp on the snow, where our oil-stove helped us a little toward comfort. It was cold, wet,

and uncomfortable; but at midnight I took
an observation, for latitude, on Polaris. The
stars were very brilliant, shedding a gentle,
reflected light on the snowy surface. This
was the first time I had succeeded in taking
an observation, as the midnight sun had
been too brilliant before, and the stars consequently dim.

The next morning, looking ahead, the
old snowy surface seemed passable; but as
soon as the grade increased we were forced
to give it up, the new snow not being
hard enough to bear our weight, and too
deep to struggle through. Our eyes were
troubling us badly, despite our goggles,
about this time; and we made a temporary
camp on a bare spot of rocks under the
cliff. With one man I again went ahead
to prospect a route, and had almost given
it up; but taking advantage of a lead
around a huge detached piece of ice, we
gained new hope, and went up to the first
crevasse. We crossed by a very narrow
and dangerous ice-bridge, with the aid of
a rope, and found a branch of the lower
crevasse heading against the main one, and
forming an acute angle in the shape of
an irregular K, the intersection being very
narrow, and a perpendicular wall of snow
overhanging at the upper angle. We cut

our way right through this snow-wall, and after a little tough climbing reached the top of the exposed cliff. Letting down about one hundred feet of rope, we made it fast to some large bowlders, and soon descended to camp, where a hot cup of coffee rewarded us for our exertion.

The next day we climbed up the cliff, and hauled up our outfit. Here, after many set-backs and tumbles, we succeeded in reaching another small glacial stream, and judged ourselves about eight miles from the summit of Elias, at an elevation of five thousand feet.

On Aug. 22 we started in earnest our climb toward the summit. The slope was gradual, but everything was a line of pure white; neither light nor shadow was apparent. One of our party called out that he couldn't see, but was afterward comforted when he found that we were all in an equally bad case, being obliged to thrust our alpenstocks in front of us to see whether or no we were going up a slope or down a hollow.

We found some immense crevasses here, from five hundred to one thousand feet in depth. Huge pendent icicles with prismatic hues and crystals of ice of every color reflected their tips on the glassy slopes. Here, looking back, we had a beautiful view over the old snow on the lower slopes, with a yellowish tinge like

Hubbard Glacier.

rich cream, while the new snow around us was dry, mealy, and white as the purest flour. Snow halos and banners hovered round Cook and other peaks, and in their changing color and shadow rivalled, if not surpassed, anything of the kind I had ever before witnessed. The scene changed almost in a moment ; and the storm-clouds went skurrying by, spreading a black mantle over the white surface. The snow began falling, for we had reached an elevation by aneroid of nine thousand feet. Above us, about five thousand feet, was the peak, which sloped at an angle of thirty degrees to a low saddle, the crest of the main range. We judged the divide to be two thousand five hundred feet above us. This was the point we desired to reach, and camp in for the night. All our hard work was over. The ice-falls, the deep crevasses, and rough glaciers lay behind; and nothing but the slope of the main peak, with its hard and regular crust of snow, lay ahead. We breathed a sigh of relief as we realized that our work was nearly over. However, the snow-storm increased; so we descended to our camp at the glacial lake, caching all our instruments at the highest point.

The storm continued to increase, and in the morning the snow had drifted nearly over our tent. Our little glacial lake had frozen, and was completely covered by the drift. The storm still raged; but at noon, a lull occurring, we decided to pull out, and return to a lower camp for more provisions. We took turns in breaking our way through the snow, barely able in the mist to see our hands before our faces, and absolutely wading through the heavy drifts. We advanced very slowly for fear of a

covered crevasse, and six in the evening
found us under the cliff; but it was still too
foggy to discover the snow-steps. We dug
a hole about ten feet square and about six
feet deep in the snow, and pitching our
tent, crawled in. The next morning it
partly cleared, and we found ourselves just
about two hundred and fifty feet from the
ice-steps. Here, letting myself down with
a rope, I recut the steps in the snow; and
after a hard struggle through the drifts we
reached our former camp at the foot of
the cliff, and were soon as comfortable as
the circumstances permitted.

After due deliberation I determined to
return, with Mr. Russell, to the upper
camp, and again attempt Elias; while the
other men, Lindsly and Stamy, were sent
to our cache at Camp 4 for more provisions and oil. The boys left us quite early,
as they had about twenty miles to make;
and we, taking our time, clambered up the
cliff, and arrived at our old "dugout" in
the snow about noon. We stopped here
to take a rest, but discovered that the oil
was dangerously low; and as the burning
of grease with improvised wicks was a
slow and unsatisfactory arrangement, I determined to leave Russell to pursue alone
the two miles to the upper lake, and pushed

back to reach our men at the lower camp. I felt in fine condition, and travelled at a dog-trot down-hill over the hard snow surface, and overtook the boys in camp below, going over the distance in six hours. Here I found a can of oil, and shared their bed and supper. We tried to get a little sleep, but were awakened by a sudden rain-storm, which started about three o'clock in the morning. We were forced to get up, cold and wet; but, making a fire out of the wooden box protecting the oil-can, ate our ham and beans with great gusto. Leaving the boys to pursue their journey to Camp 4, I started back to reach Russell. It got colder and colder as I advanced. The wind and rain blew in my face, and soon soaked through my rubber clothing. I became like a wet rag. At the first ice-fall it was sleeting, and I had some difficulty in climbing the steep and icy slopes with my heavy pack. I reached our old camp under the cliff at five P.M. Resting a moment, I climbed up the rocky wall, and reached the upper slope. Here it was snowing fiercely in great flakes. I trudged ahead, but soon every vestige of our old trail was covered, and I wallowed in the deep snow. It was then about six P.M.; and fearing that I might be buried here in the depth of snow, I made the best of my way back to the lower camp. I reached the cliff about eight o'clock, the storm being terrific in force. I tugged at the rope, but found it caught at the bottom, so I kept on my pack, and clambered down. At best, the cliff was a nasty place; and loaded as I was, and tired out, I slipped while half-way down, and turned to grasp the rope. I could not hold on, so fell headlong the rest of the distance. A flashing thought of the hard ice and deep crevasse at the bottom was obscured in my surprise at landing in soft snow. I soon got up, shook myself, and finding no bones broken, made the best of my way to the old camp. The weight of the new snow had caused an avalanche, burying the end of the rope, and filling the crevasse at the bottom. This had happened since my last trip, — a lucky accident, and to it I owe my life. At my camp was a rubber blanket; so, bracing it with an alpenstock, I made an improvised tent, the ends being fastened with large snowballs; the snow rapidly filled in round my tent, and I was soon comfortably sleeping. I woke up hungry during the night, and finding a little oatmeal, made a hasty-pudding, which appeased my appetite a little.

Early the next morning (the 27th) the temperature rose, and it began to rain. Then my troubles began. Everything was absolutely soaking. I did not mind it much during the day, but as the night grew colder I soon became benumbed. I kept up the circulation as much as possible, but was so stiff in the morning that I could scarcely move. Luckily it cleared; and the sun coming out, I stretched out my hands toward its genial rays, and could readily imagine how men could bow down in silent adoration of such glorious warmth. New strength and energy were imparted into my frozen limbs. I found my feet and hands a little frost-bitten, but plunged them at intervals in the snow. I had time to dry out somewhat before attempting to reach Russell, two miles above, where I knew food and warmth awaited me. Thirty hours on raw oatmeal I soon found was not travelling diet through soft snow about four feet deep; so after going half a mile I was forced to give it up, and return again to my camp. As I lay there in my snowy camp, I began to wonder if I should be found in future ages, preserved in glacier ice like a mammoth or cave-bear, as an illustration to geologists that man inhabited these regions of eternal ice, and lived happily on nothing, breathing the free air of prehistoric times.

Soon it became quite cold; and, dreaming of more delightful scenes, I heard a shout, and in a little while four of the men came in with supplies. I took a piece of chocolate and corned beef, and felt better. They had been delayed by the storm, and were anxious about our safety. We made a cup of beef-tea over an improvised lamp, which braced me considerably. We started the next day (the 29th), quite early, to reach Russell, as we imagined he might be a little lonely. We forced our way through the snow, and about half-way met him slowly coming toward us, bringing a light load. Sending two men to his camp for the tent and oil-stove, we again moved back to our camp at the cliff.

The snow in these two storms had fallen and drifted to the depth of about nine feet, and was so soft that one sunk almost to the waist in attempting to push through it, and we had no proper snow-shoes. The winter had actually set in, and we realized we were too late to reach our instruments and again attempt the peak. It was severely disappointing, after days of travel over rough moraines and icy glaciers, crossing by narrow bridges, hauling ourselves up steep cliffs and precipices, swimming streams, and living for weeks with an oil-stove for fuel, sleeping four abreast in a 7×7 tent on the snow; in fact, six weeks of utter discomfort for body and soul, and then to be beaten by so little! If the storm had only held off for twenty-four hours more, the scalp of Elias would have been in our belt, and we could have finished the trip with great rejoicing. However, our attempt was bold, and our success in finding and naming new peaks and glaciers, and studying their movements, and, indeed, making a general topographical reconnoissance of this unknown region, recompensed us in part for the failure in reaching the summit of Elias. So turning our backs on the mountain, we returned to our base camp at Blossom Island during another storm, and tried to forget our disappointment in eating bear-meat and wild huckleberries.

The rest of the season I was engaged in extending the topographical work; and in one of these trips I went down to the Indian village and met the Corwin, with my friend Captain C. L. Hooper in command. Learning of our trips up the bay, he set sail, and, landing at the entrance to

Disenchantment Bay, brought off the remainder of the party. The Corwin thus had the honor of being the first vessel to steam up Yakutat Bay. We stayed only a few hours at the village at Port Mulgrave, and after a delightful voyage reached Port Townsend on Oct. 2, our party disbanded, and the men all returned to their various homes.

A THOUSAND MILES THROUGH THE ALPS

By Sir W. Martin Conway

Morning—from a summit.

HEN I began climbing mountains, almost a quarter of a century ago, mountaineering —at all events in the Alps— was a very different matter from what it is to-day. The age of Alpine conquest was even then approaching its close; but present conditions did not prevail, and the sentiment of climbers was still that of pioneers.

The old-fashioned climber, the mountain hero of my boyhood, was a traveller, and desired to be an explorer. When he went to the Alps, he went to wander about and to rough it. Many peaks were still unclimbed, and by most people conceived to be unclimbable. He probably thought he could reduce the number, and it was his chief ambition to do so. The desire to discover new routes, which still lingers among Alpine travellers, is a belated survival from the days when all the Alps were unclimbed. The rush of tourists that came with improved means of communication, and was accompanied by a development of railways, roads, and inns throughout the frequented and more accessible parts of Switzerland, could not be without effect upon mountaineering. The change showed itself chiefly in this respect, that the habitual climber, the man for whom Alpine climbing takes the place of another's fishing or shooting, ceased to be a traveller, and acquired the habit of settling down for the whole time of his holiday in a comfortably furnished centre, whence he makes a series of ascents of the high mountains within its reach.

Previously mountaineering was one of the best forms of training for a traveller, and indeed supplied for busy persons, whose annual holiday must be short, experience of all the charms, excitements, and delights which reward the explorer of distant and unknown regions of the earth. The object of the journey now to be described was to discover whether the time had not come when a return might be made, on a novel footing, to the habits of Alpine pioneers. Of course the mystery is gone from the Alps, — none but climbers know how completely. Every mountain and point of view of even third-rate importance has been ascended, most by many routes. Almost every gap between two peaks has been traversed as a pass. The publications of some dozen mountaineering societies have recorded these countless expeditions in rows of volumes of appalling length. Of late years vigorous attempts have been made to coördinate this mass of material in the form of Climbers' Guides, dealing with particular districts, wherein every peak and pass is dealt with in strict geographical succession, and every different route, and all the variations of each route, are set forth, with references to the volumes in which they have been described at length by their discoverers. Nearly half the Alps has been treated in this manner; but the work has taken ten years, and of course the whole requires periodical revision.

It occurred to me that it was now possible, taking the whole range of the Alps, to devise a route, or rather a combination of climbs, the descent from each ending at the starting-point for the next, such that one might begin at one extremity of the snowy range and walk up and down through its midst to the other extremity over a continuous series of peaks and passes. The Alps, of course, though spoken of as a range, are not a single line of peaks, but a series of locally parallel ridges covering a region. There is no continuous Alpine ridge at all that stretches from one end of the region to the other. It would be possible to devise an almost infinite variety of combinations of peaks and passes that would fulfil the conditions of my plan. Some of these would take years to carry out, for they would lead over peaks that can only be ascended under exceptionally good conditions of weather. The route selected had to be capable of execution within three months of average weather — a mixture of good and bad, with the bad predominating. It was also essential that it should lead continuously through snowy regions, and that it should traverse as many of the more interesting and well-known groups as possible.

By beginning with the smaller ranges at the southern extremity of the Alpine

region we were able to start early in the summer season with the maximum of time before us. The Colle di Tenda, over which goes the road from Turin to Ventimiglia, is regarded as the southern limit of the Alps, and the boundary between them and the Apennines. Thither, therefore, we transferred ourselves on June 1. The first division of the journey was thence to Mont Blanc, which, of course, had to be traversed; this line of route lay partly in France, but chiefly in Italy, the Dauphiny mountains being of necessity omitted as lying apart in an isolated group. At Mont Blanc we had to decide between two main possible ways. We might go along the southern Pennine, Lepontine, and other ranges, or by the northern Oberland ridge and its eastward continuations. I chose the northern route as being the shorter and, to me, more novel. Arriving thus at the eastern extremity of Switzerland, the general line to be followed across the Tyrol was obvious, the final goal being the

Ankogel, the last snowy peak in the direction of Vienna, about a hundred and eighty miles from that city.

The party assembled at the Colle di Tenda for this expedition was rather a large one as Alpine parties go. I was fortunate to secure as companion my friend Mr. E. A. Fitzgerald, an experienced climber, who has since won distinction as an explorer in the snow-mountains of New Zealand. He brought with him two well-known guides, J. B. Aymonod and Louis Carrel, both of Valtournanche, a village near the south foot of the Matterhorn. Carrel is famous as one of the guides who accompanied Mr. Whymper to the Andes. For the first part of the journey I engaged my old Himalayan companion, the guide Mattias Zurbriggen, of Macugraga; and I was further accompanied by two of the Gurkhas (natives of Nepal) who were with me in the Himalayas, to wit, Lance Naick Amar Sing Thapa and Lance Naick Karbir Bura Thoki, both of the first battalion of the Fifth Gurkha Rifles. The Gurkhas are admirable scramblers and good weight-carriers, but they were not experienced in the craft of climbing snow-mountains. They had begun to learn the use of the axe and rope in India;

Halt at the Top of a slope   Gurkhas and Swiss Guide.

but it was felt that if they could spend a
further period of three months, working
under first-rate guides, their mountaineering education would be advanced, and they
would be better able on their return to
India to assist in Himalayan exploration,
up till now so neglected.   It was in view
of giving them experience of snow and

glacier work that our route was devised to
keep as far as possible to snow, and to
avoid rather than seek rock-scrambling, in
which they were already proficient.

Fortunate people who live on islands, or
without bellicose neighbors, have no idea
of the excitements of frontier travel in
central Europe. As long as you merely
want to cross from one country into another, there is only the custom-house nui-
sance to be fought through; but try to
settle down near a frontier and enjoy yourself in a normal fashion, walking to pretty
points of view, and staring about as you
please, all sorts of annoyances and impedi-
ments start in your way; while if you wish
to travel along the frontier, these become
indefinitely multiplied. It is useless to
dodge gendarmes and folks of that kidney
on the Franco-Italian frontier. They are
too numerous, active, and suspicious. We
knew this, and made what we supposed
were sufficient arrangements beforehand.
Ministers and august personages were approached by one or another on our behalf,
friendly promises were given, and the way
seemed smooth before us; but we started
along it too soon, not bearing in mind that
governmental machineries, though they
may ultimately grind exceeding small, do

so with phenomenal slowness. When, therefore, we actually came upon frontier ground, we were not expected, and the ways were often closed against us. It was not till just as we were leaving Italy for the unsuspicious and more travelled regions of Savoy and Switzerland that the spreading wave of orders and recommendations in our favor, washing outward from the official centre, broke against the mountain-wall, and produced a sudden profusion of kindnesses and attentions which, if they had come a fortnight sooner, would have made our journey more pleasant.

As it was, however, we were treated in the Maritime and Cottian Alps as probable spies. The peaks and passes we wanted to climb were closed against us; and we had continually to change our plans in order to avoid fortresses and the like futilities, sight of which in the far distance without permission is a crime. Nor were these political difficulties the only ones we had to contend against in the first part of our journey. Eager to be early on the ground, we arrived too early. None of the inns were open in the upper valleys, and the high pastures and huts were all deserted; so that we had to descend low for food, and often to sleep in the open air. Moreover, to make matters worse, the season was backward. The mass of winter snow had waited till May to fall, and in June the mountains were draped with a vesture proper to the month of March. Ascents were thereby rendered dangerous from avalanches, or even impossible, which should have been little more than grass walks. It was, therefore, in every sense a misfortune that our start was not delayed at least a fortnight.

With every disadvantage, however, we saw enough of the Maritime Alps to gain a fair idea of their scenery, which is superb, and differs in character from that of other Alpine regions. Their greatest charm is derived from their situation between the Mediterranean on the one side, and the Lombard plain on the other, broad, level expanses toward which mountain buttresses gracefully descend. Ill-luck in weather deprived us of the choicest views; yet there is a beauty in cloud-enframed glimpses perhaps no less great than the clearest prospect can afford. The mountains do not rise to any great height; and though their summits and gullies hold snow all the year round, it is not in quantity sufficient to form glaciers. But the valleys are so deep that for a climber the altitudes to be ascended are

A Thousand Miles through the Alps

Cloud Effect on Glacier.

as great as in the case of the high peaks of
the central Alps. The scrambling is good;
for the range is chiefly built of limestone,
which presents difficult problems of a gymnastic character. The valleys possess a singular charm; for they are richly wooded,
and the streams that enliven them are of
clear water dancing down in crystal floods.
Moreover, the color of the atmosphere is
richer than in Switzerland and the Tyrol,
so that hollows are filled with bluer shadows, distances are softer, and floating clouds
receive an added tenderness.

Rather more than three weeks were
spent in travelling from the sea to Mont
Blanc. The principal peaks climbed on
the way were Monte Viso and the Aiguille
de la Grande-Sassière, the one in storm,
the other on a perfect day. It is a mis-
take to imagine that mountain scenery is
only beautiful in fine weather. It is often
more impressive in fog or storm than at
any other time. Clouds, which shut out
the distance, force the eye to linger on the
foreground of ice and rock, which possess
beauties of their own. It is not for mere
summit panoramas that lovers of scenery
are led to climb. Every stage of ascent
and descent gives its own reward. Monte
Viso, when we climbed it, was not the

naked rock-peak known to summer travellers. It was buried deep in hard, frozen snow, which the violent gale swept into the air, and whirled about in twisted wreaths. Clouds, too, were dragged across it, and, as it were, combed through the teeth of its serrated rock-ridge. Few wilder or more impressive scenes have I witnessed than that we beheld from near the top of the peak when the gale was at its height. The air seemed to be writhing about us. We were all covered with frozen filaments; icicles hung from our hair. We had to cling to the rocks or be blown away. Such moments of excitement may at the time be physically disagreeable ; but they are morally stimulating in a high degree, and linger in the memory far more agreeably than do afternoons of slothful dalliance and luxurious repose.

As we travelled forward from day to day the peaks we were to climb first appeared in the remote distance, then coming nearer, separated themselves from their fellows, till at last each in its turn blocked the way, and had to be climbed over. Mont Blanc was long a-coming. We saw it first from the Sassière, as a culminating dome above a lower wall of neighbors. Next we saw it while descending the

A Storm on Mount Viso — forced to cling to the rock or be blown away

Maritime Alps at Dawn.

Ruitor Glacier. That morning the clouds were low, and for hours we saw nothing that was not near at hand. The Ruitor snow-field is large and gently inclined. We had to steer our way down it by compass and map. Its white rippled surface spread around us, melting at the edges of vision into a sparkling mist which the sunlight illuminated, but was long in driving away. At last there came a movement in the fog, a strange twinkling and flickering as of ghosts passing by. Uncertain forms appeared and vanished. Low, striking light-bands striped the white floor. Suddenly, to our bewildered delight, there stood, behind a faint veil which swiftly melted away, the whole Mont Blanc range, clear from end to end, superb in form, and glittering in sunshine. Entranced, we halted to gaze as the fairy vision hardened into reality.

A couple of days later we were on the mountain itself, approaching its snowy region by way of the Miage Glacier, which lies in a deep and splendid valley. We spent the night in a hut on the great peak's flank, but started on again by one o'clock in the morning, so as to traverse the steep snow-slopes to the ridge while frost held them firm. The progress from night to day in this remote snowy fastness went forward as we ascended, and the sun had risen when we stood on the frontier ridge which was to be followed to the top. Already Europe was at our feet. The ranges by which we had come stretched southward into blue vagueness; on the other side were the green hills of Savoy, the hollow of Geneva's lake, and I know not what far-stretching plains and undulations of France. Looking along the ridge, the Aiguille de Bionassay, a splendid pyramid

A Thousand Miles through the Alps

The Slopes on either Side are Steep

of snow, passing graceful, and edged with delicately sharpened ice-ridges, divided the two views from one another. We turned our backs on the pyramid and climbed ahead, following a crest of snow, sometimes sharp as an axe-edge, often curled over like a breaking wave on one side or the other. As snow *arêtes* go, this one is not remarkable for narrowness; but the slopes on either hand are steep, and have the usual appearance of precipitance. Hence it was that in August, 1890, Count Umberto di Villanova, with his famous guides Antonio Castagneri and J. J. Maquignaz, were blown to destruction by a violent gale. Their bodies were never found, but their footsteps were traced to this point. On which side of the ridge they fell we have no means of knowing.

By noon we stood on the culminating point of the Alps, the first visitors of the year. Since my former visit a hut had been set up in this desolate spot, — a disfigurement, but a useful shelter, — beneath which we took refuge from a chilly wind. Clouds decorated without obliterating the glorious panorama, beyond question the finest in the Alps, and surpassed only, if at all in Europe, by that from Caucasian Elbruz. Flocks of cloudlets grazed the green

Along the Snow Arête.

hills at our feet, and lines of small soft billows, as it were breaking on a wide and shallow shore, undulated in the remote distance. The sky, for a quarter of its height, had parted with its blue to the valley deeps, and was striped around with fine horizontal lines, each edging a new grade of tone, like the lines in a solar spectrum. We ran down to Chamonix by the historic route. The sun blazed upon us, and the heat was intolerable; but toward evening a copper-colored tower of cloud arose in the west, and cast a solemn shadow on the glacier.

It was night when we reached the valley, and we entered Chamonix in the dark.

If we had now taken the southern route, we should have had a fine series of glacier passes to cross from Chamonix to Zermatt; but all of them were well known to me, and I preferred a new region. So we went through the limestone Savoy hills, over small peaks and passes, easy enough to traverse, but delightful for the variety of scenery and its swift changes of character. It was not till we had crossed the Rhone valley and climbed the Diablerets that large glaciers came much in our way. Each day we climbed a peak, and descended to some cowherd's hut to sleep. They were all dirty, so that we often chose rather to lie on the grass in the open air than to shelter within them. Valseret was the worst. We reached it as the cows came jangling home to be milked. The peasants gathered round a fire near the door to eat their evening meal of hard bread and *maigre* cheese, which they toasted on the embers. Swarms of flies came with them. The men crammed their mouths full of food, and then shouted at the cows, who were butting one another all around. The wind whisked ashes into their eyes, but nothing disturbed their stolid equanimity. The meal ended, each hid his loaf and cheese in a hole in the wall. The cows meanwhile looked in and snorted, eager to be milked. No one spoke, and only the flies were gay. The surroundings of the hut were incredibly foul, and we had to go some distance to find a clean spot to sleep on.

·The finest scenery in this part of our journey, at the west end of the famous Bernese Oberland, was that of the glacier of the great Dead Plain. We did not see it until we were on its edge, and the white expanse spread before us. It fills a kind of elliptical hollow, some two miles long by a mile wide. Once on its smooth, large surface, the external world is shut out by a ring of low mountain wall. Not a trace of human activity can be seen in any direction. The largeness, simplicity, and seclusion of this strange snow-field made it unique. We traversed its longest diameter. The snow, fortunately, remained hard throughout the hour of our passage, thanks to a cool breeze and a veiled sun. The surface was beautifully rippled and perfectly clean.

A few days farther on we came to the chief mass of Oberland mountains, the Jungfrau and her fellows. Right through the heart of the range goes a splendid

A Snow Cornice.

snow-valley, cut across at three places by
low passes, but orographically continuous. Two days' marching took us from
end to end of this longest snow traverse
in the Alps. We halted for two nights in
the midst of it at the Concordia hut by
the snow-field of the Great Aletsch glacier, and spent the intervening day in
ascending the Jungfrau. Few European
mountains are easier or more beautiful,

for the starting-point is remote from the habitations of man, and all the climb is done in one of Nature's purest and most enclosed solitudes. Rocks are not once touched between the Concordia hut and the summit; the whole route lies over spotless snow and ice, up gently inclined plains of it, and then steeper slopes to a ridge of ice, and so to the top. The views are throughout of snowy regions, and not till the summit is gained does the sight plunge down to fertile valleys, blue lakes, and a far-off land of woods and fields. As we stood on the highest point, and looked over the great snow-basin to the towering Finsteraarhorn, with a bright roof of cirrus cloud spread above it on the blue sky, I thought I had seldom beheld a more impressive spectacle.

Thus far the weather, though by no means perfect, and often bad, had not been systematically evil; but from this time forward our journey was made in a succession of storms, separated from one another by thinnest fine-weather partitions. On one perfect day we climbed the Galenstock, a mountain known to all who have crossed the Furka. We left the Grimsel inn before midnight, and came in a dark hour to the pallid snow-field of the Rhône Glacier. Crossing it, as in a featureless dream, we mounted a monotonous snowy valley to the mountain's ridge, where such a splendor of dawn burst upon us from the glowing east that it obliterates all other memories, and remains the feature of the day. We looked abroad over low Italian and Ticino hills, bathed in soft air and transparent mist, and playing at hide-and-seek with floating lines and balls of changeful cloud; then on to the Engadine peaks, and farther yet to remote ranges under a newly risen sun, forming backgrounds to the various-tinted atmosphere, through which each, remoter than the ridge before, seemed more soft and ethereal than its neighbor, till the last led fitly to the sky.

Looking back, however, upon this part of our journey — the traverse, that is to say, from the Oberland into the Tyrol — it stands out as a period of storm. We went forward without regard to weather, and took what came. Sometimes we started in fog, and steered by compass and map to the glacier, then felt our way up it to some narrow pass by which access was obtained to the next valley. These were exciting times. One day, for instance, we had to cross the Silvretta group of mountains in the neighborhood of the

Lower Engadine. We had been unable to obtain the least glimpse of them, so dense were the clouds that enveloped them. Yet we started at our usual hour in the morning, trusting to luck and an indifferent map as guide. For hours the way was up a swampy valley that bent and branched with fitful vagrance. Avoiding wrong turns, we came to a glacier's foot which loomed forth out of the fog and rain. We advanced up it not without satisfaction, for physical features on a glacier are more orderly in sequence than they are in a mere upland valley; and the character of the snow under foot reveals the level attained, an element by which to reckon the way.

Getting down a rock crevice.

The rain presently gave place to falling snow, which the wind drove against us. We could not see twenty yards in any direction. At the foot of the glacier we took the bearing of the pass; but the map we had was twenty years old, and in the interval the glacier had greatly changed, so that the bearing was not correct. Roping in a long line for convenience of guiding, the compass-bearer being last, we set forward at a late hour of the afternoon into the wild upper regions. The new snow under foot was soft and deep. For hours we waded, rather than walked upward. Only the dip of the slope we were on, and the barometric altitude, gave indication of the place we had reached. Higher and higher we went, hoping to run into the gap; but only the slope rose featureless before us, to vanish in fog a few yards away. Daylight waned, and still the advance continued. The barometer showed that we were far above the level of the pass. We had missed it, therefore, and were climbing a peak beside it; but was the pass on our left hand or on our right? Probably the right, we said; so we struck off that way, and traversed horizontally, then up again, and then another traverse. The gale raged wildly, the snow whirled in our faces, and buffeted us into a stupid condition. At last a tooth of rock came in view close at hand, and we knew we must be near the ridge. A few minutes later we were going down the other side like wild creatures, racing for

In Wind and Snow.

the day. Half an hour brought us suddenly into clear air, and showed us a green
valley leading down, and mountains at the
end of it, on which the evening light was
beginning to fade. We ran down the valley to the long slope at its mouth, and in
the dark night we plunged and stumbled
through a pathless wood to the Engadine
highroad at its foot.

This was but one of many similar experiences. Sometimes the evening was

fine, sometimes the morning, but the rest of the day was usually given over to storm. We became callous as time went on, and the habit of bad-weather travelling grew in us. There are certainly excitements and beautiful effects as well which are only to be had in mountains in bad weather, and these we enjoyed to the full. Wild places, such as the lofty secluded rock-bound lake of Mutt in Canton Glarus, never look so fine as when clouds are rolling over them.

On the way to the Mutt Lake we had a strange adventure, of which I was fortunate enough to secure a photograph. We were approaching the highest sheep pasture as the day waned. The sheep, seventeen hundred in number, saw us from the surrounding slopes, and, urged by a longing for salt, rushed down upon us from all sides, with one united " Baa," in a wild converging avalanche. We beat off the leaders, but they could not retreat, for those behind pressed them forward. Finding that Carrel was the saltest morsel, the whole flock surged upon him. They lifted him off his feet, carried him forward, cast him to the ground, and poured over him. Fortunately the ground was flat. When the shepherd saw what had happened he whistled shrilly thrice, whereupon the sheep dispersed in terror, fleeing up the mountain-side in all directions, till no two remained together.

At Nauders we entered the Tyrol, that happy hunting-ground of the German and Austrian Alpine Club, a body whose popularity and power may be gauged by the fact that it possesses over thirty thousand members, and its activity by the hundred and odd climbers' huts it has built, the footpaths it has made, the inns it has subsidized, the thousands of spots of paint it has splashed upon rocks, and finger-posts it has set up by waysides to indicate the wanderers' route. The contrast between Switzerland and the Tyrol, from a traveller's point of view, consists herein, that whereas travel in Switzerland is exploited by hotel-keepers and organized in their interests, the Tyrol is, through the agency of the powerful German and Austrian Alpine Club, organized by travellers themselves in their own interests. In Switzerland traps are laid for the tourist's francs; in the Tyrol every effort is made to spare his pocket. The Tyrol is thus the paradise of poor holiday-makers, who wander impartially over the whole country, nine out of ten of them carrying their own

Getting Down a Glacier.

packs, and enjoying themselves in a reasonable and decent fashion.

Every one who has climbed a Swiss mountain knows what a *cabane* is like. It is usually a rough stone hut, perhaps divided by wooden partitions into two or three chambers. In a corner of one is a small stove. On a shelf are a few pots, plates, cups, and a crooked set of odd knives, forks, and spoons. In the other room are beds of hay ranged along the floor, and sometimes also on shelves. The stove smokes. The door has to be left open or the fire will not draw. Draughts find their way in through numerous chinks. Early in the season the floor is probably covered with ice. Ancient and fusty rugs form the sole bed-covering. The newer huts, built by the Italian Alpine Club, are an improvement on these horrid Swiss shelters. They are framed of well-fitted wood; and all their appointments are better, but they consist of the same elements.

In the case of Mont Blanc alone, on the rocks called the Grands-Mulets, there is a hut where a woman resides to act as attendant and cook. Even this *cabane* is a wretched hole, dirty, draughty, and uncomfortable in more ways than can be briefly catalogued. The climber on this route up Mont Blanc can, indeed, sleep in a bed, procure a hot meal, and purchase provisions; but his bill for indifferent accommodation and food will come to about a hundred francs, the bulk of which goes, not to the innkeeper, but, in the form of rent, to the Commune of Chamonix. Compare the Grands-Mulets with such a

(pp 347-48)

Interior of a Hut in the Tyrol (Kurninger Hut).

Tyrolese hut as the Warnsdorfer. The comparison is fair; for the height of both is about the same, as is also their distance from the nearest village. This hut is a wooden building of two stories on a massive base, to which it is bound with steel cables. On the ground floor are a kitchen and guides' room, a dining-room, and some bedrooms. Up-stairs are more bedrooms, and a hayloft for the guides. A clean little woman lives in the place to do the cooking and service, and extend a warm welcome to the traveller, who can, at any hour, procure from her a hot meal of fresh meat well prepared. He can buy wine or liquors. He can write a letter and post it. He can amuse himself in the skittle alley outside the door, or play at chess, cards, or other games within. The bedrooms are clean and well furnished. They are provided with fireplaces. In the dining-room, which is warmed, are chairs and tables, with tablecloths, books, a clock, a barometer, a guitar, pen and ink, pictures, maps, and various other conveniences, besides a cupboard containing an elaborate medical and surgical apparatus. A member of any Alpine Club whatever pays two-pence for the use of the hut by day, and about a shilling for his bed at night. Provisions are correspondingly cheap. Guides do not pay for lodgings, and are supplied with food at an economical rate.

Huts of the first order, like this one, are becoming numerous. Each is the property of one of the local sections of the German Club, and generally bears its name,— the Magdeburg Hut, the Brunswick Hut, the Dresden Hut, and so on. Sections try to outdo one another in the excellence of the accommodation they provide, and every year sees some improvement. One day, when we were crossing through the midst of the Stubai Mountains in a dense fog (as usual), guiding ourselves merely by the compass, there suddenly came a cave in the clouds, and in the midst of it appeared a large stone house in course of erection, planted on the top of a rocky eminence rising out of the snow-field. It is the last new thing in huts, and when finished will be really a hotel, capable of accommodating at least fifty guests. Such elaborate *cabanes* are not yet numerous, but in the next few years they will spread over the whole snowy area of the Tyrol. After them come huts of the second order, in which no attendant resides, but where supplies can be obtained. Each of these huts contains its store of firewood, frequently renewed, and a cupboard full of tinned meats, tea, sugar, compressed soups, wine, spirits, and even champagne. The prices of these things are posted up on the wall. There are mattresses and bedding. Often there are books, maps, and games. The

Street of a Mountain Village.

traveller supplies himself with what he pleases, makes out his own bill, writes it in a book, and deposits the money in a box, which is as often as not unlocked. Yet a third order of huts is to be found. They for the most part occupy the most elevated situations, close to the summits of peaks, or on the saddles of passes, and are intended merely as refuges from storms. They resemble ordinary Swiss huts, to the average of which they are usually superior ; like them they contain no supplies. The present tendency is to rebuild these on a larger scale, and provide them with stores.

The Tyrol is as much ahead of Switzerland in climber's food as it is in mountain huts. Who does not know the stringy meat and hard cheese that form the staple contents of a Swiss mountaineer's wallet? If he is a careful and foreseeing person, perhaps he provides himself with a tin or two of American beef or fruit. But the average Tyrolese climber would regard his best hillside *menu* with scorn. In the Tyrol it is seldom necessary to carry any provisions except bread. There are two or three huts on most mountains, and you call at them for your meals. In many, and a year or two hence probably in all, you will find baskets stocked according to what they call the " Pottsche Provian " system. From these you can supply yourself with a meal in several courses, and you have your choice of two or three wines. The various tins contain elaborate and excellent messes of food, some to be heated before served. It would be hard to cite a more elaborate and successful application of the coöperative principle to the supply of commodities. The German and Austrian Alpine Club is in reality a coöperative association of over thirty thousand members, who kindly permit the members of other Alpine clubs to participate in their advantages.

When it is remembered that the guide-system of the Tyrol is under the governance of this club, that it makes paths, receives privileges from the railways, publishes and supplies gratis to its members useful annuals, maps superior to those provided by the government surveys, and handbooks of different sorts, the value and extent of its activity may be conceived. The whole country is in consequence wandered over, not by herds of tourists following personal conductors, but by an immense number of individuals going alone or in parties of two or three, taking a guide now and again from one hut to another, but for the most part carrying their own baggage and finding their own way. There are no great centres where people flock together and make one another miserable. Travellers keep moving about, and strew themselves fairly evenly over the mountain area.

Each hut and village inn forms a small focus where chance assemblages of wanderers meet for the night, to sunder again next day. Community of momentary interests unites them into a society for the few hours of their common life. The wandering spirit pervades them and the whole country during the summer season. Twenty years ago this state of things did not exist. I remember the Stubai and Zillerthal Mountains when there was not a hut among them, not a guide nor an ice-axe in their villages. During the three months I spent in the district, scarcely a traveller came by. The change, which is due to German enterprise, is doubtless re-acting upon the youth of Germany. The spirit cultivated by the mediæval *Wander-schaft*, which sent every young craftsman away from his home for three years, now grows out of the annual summer tramp. Youthful students from the German uni-versities are infected by it. They range like mediæval roving scholars in their hun-dreds over the land, and penetrate the mountain regions. All the huts and most of the inns open their arms to receive them at reduced rates, so that a lad with a few florins in his pocket can wander unre-strained from place to place.

Hannove's Hut at Ankogel.

The picture which I have thus endeavored to draw will present little attraction, no doubt, to most of my readers. Comfortable hotels, in the usual European sense, do not await them here. There are few carriage-roads in the best parts of the country. The place is not arranged for their convenience. It is designed for the fairly robust wanderer, who goes his way without a plan, and desires only to find at suitable times a roof over his head, sound food to eat, and splendid scenery to delight the eye and develop the imagination. Such a one, especially if he possesses some mountaineering experience and capacity, may traverse the mountain region, in company with a like-minded friend or two, from north to south, and from east to west, ascending snowy peaks and crossing glacier passes, without requiring the assistance of either guide or porter. In every group of mountains he will find huts placed in the best positions for scenery, not in the likeliest places for entrapping guests. Everywhere he will meet a free and intelligent, if sometimes a rather rough and boisterous company. He will seldom find himself either solitary or overcrowded. He will suffer more from well-intended kindness than from rudeness or neglect. He

will never be swindled. In fine, no part
of the Alps now forms a better training-
ground for the youthful would-be mountaineer, none a less vulgarized holiday
resort for the man of moderate physical
capabilities, simple tastes, or restricted
means, than the region comprised in the
Austrian and Bavarian Tyrol.